SECRET PLEASURE

THE SECRET SERIES

JILL SANDERS

GRAYTON

To all my good friends,
past and present

Jennifer
Cyndi
Monica
Jeannie
Carmen
Shannon
Essie
Melinda
Nancy
Tiffany
Marcella
Crystal

Just to list a few...

SUMMARY

After a terrible breakup and the loss of her dream job, Airlea is just looking for a fresh start. When her mother takes it upon herself to help, Airlea finds herself working for a wealthy family back in Italy, whose son was recently involved in a serious auto accident. She jumps at the chance to escape Greece and leave her worries behind, unaware of the new dangers she now faces in Rome. To further complicate things, she now must deal with the most arrogant patient she's ever seen, which would be a lot easier if he wasn't so damn sexy!

Dante is fed up with his broken body. All he wants to do is work through the pain and try to get his life back to normal. Instead, his mother hires an amazingly bossy nurse to help with his rehab, which might go a lot easier if she wasn't so damn hot! Trying to keep his nosy family out of his business and vying for the affection of his beautiful nurse could end up being a dangerous affair.

irlea walked out of the hospital just after midnight. Her shift had ended an hour earlier, but she'd been so caught up helping her latest patient, Anna, she'd been late leaving work. Anna had been in a fire just over a month ago, and seventy percent of her little, eight-year-old body had been badly burned. Her little arms and legs had the telltale signs of scarring, and even though she was still wrapped up tight in bandages, Airlea knew what was underneath them.

Getting the little girl to trust her had been easy, keeping her happy wasn't. Airlea knew the road ahead for Anna was going to be a difficult one and she knew by the time she got done, Anna wasn't going to like her. Tonight, Anna had gotten her first glimpse at what was ahead of her. Airlea had pushed the little girl until there were big fat tears rolling down her perfect little cheeks.

Being a physical therapist was what Airlea was born to do. She loved helping others heal and recover after something major had knocked them down. She looked at it as a rebirth experience for her patients. Most of them came out the other side a changed person. Almost all came out a better person than they'd been when they'd experienced their setbacks.

She was walking the same roads she'd walked for the last five years of her life. Her tiny apartment was only two blocks from the hospital in Igoumenitsa, Greece. She'd been born and raised just outside of Venice, Italy, but shortly after finishing school, she'd moved to Greece when she'd been offered a full-time position at the hospital here. She'd enjoyed her time ever since arriving.

She had friends and had even had a few relationships, her latest ending a little over a month ago. Angelo Ernesto had been everything Airlea had ever wanted in a man. He'd been caring, patient, kind, very good looking, and a doctor. That was until she'd allowed him to move in with her after they had been dating for six months. Then everything had changed.

It had taken less than a week for her to see the side of himself that he'd been hiding. The jealousy and temper brought on by the smallest things had been the reason she'd asked him to move out less than a month after he'd moved in. Now when she walked by him in the halls of the hospital, she tried to avoid talking to him.

How could something so beautiful be so rotten on the inside? She'd learned a valuable lesson with him. Angelo still called her sometimes, but she'd gotten to the point where she didn't answer his calls anymore. Every call she did answer would start out with him apologizing, then it would escalate to him raising his voice about why she wouldn't take him back. She just didn't want to deal with him anymore.

She'd made it halfway up the stairs outside her apartment before she saw Angelo sitting on the steps. She rolled her eyes; she wasn't in the mood to deal with him anymore.

"Hi," he said, standing up and matching her steps to follow her the rest of the way to her apartment door.

"Listen, Angelo, I'm really tired. I've just gotten off my shift and I'm heading straight to bed. Can we talk tomorrow, instead?" She hunted in her bag for her keys, not even glancing in his direction.

When she reached her door, he pushed her until her back was up against the hard wood, the door knob thrust painfully against her hip. His hands held her shoulders back.

"Damn it, Airlea, if you never talk to me, how can we make this all better?" He growled.

"Let go of me!" When he didn't, she dropped her bag and tried to push him back a step. He didn't budge. "We are not going to work this out. Don't you get it? I don't want to work it out. It just didn't work, move on."

"I can't believe you're being such a bitch about this. You kick me out with some lame-ass excuse and now you won't even talk to me." He held her, looking down into her eyes. "If you'd just give me a chance." He started moving his head towards her, leaning in as if he was coming in for a kiss.

She turned her head away. "Get off me, Angelo. I've told you, it's over. Get off!" She pushed him again, this time catching him off guard a little. He took two steps back and glared at her as she slid her keys in the door and quickly stepped inside, leaving her bag outside her door.

"You think this is over?" he screamed to her closed

door. "I have pull at the hospital. Don't think I won't use it." She watched him through her peep-hole as he picked up her bag and walked away. She relaxed against her locked door, very glad that the scene was over. So, she'd lost her scrubs and her extra pair of shoes. She knew she could get them back if she just talked to him, but she didn't want to, and the items didn't really matter.

The next day at work, she was called into the director's office. As she stood in front of his large metal desk, she kicked herself for the fool she was.

"Miss Rossi is this your bag?" Mr. Lutz wasn't one of those 'hands-on' kind of directors. He was strict and very old-school. Any explanation she might have given as to how he'd gotten her bag and who had taken it and why, would fall on deaf ears.

"Yes, sir." She braced herself for whatever was going to come next.

"Can you explain this?" He opened the bag and she watched as a dozen pill bottles fell out. She recognized some of the names on the labels and her mouth fell open. The bottles of medicine had been missing for over a week. Employees of the hospital had received memos all week long about the missing medication.

An hour later she walked out of the hospital, the contents of her locker in a box tucked under her arm, and her dignity lost forever. She assured herself the entire short walk home that she would never trust a man again.

Dante threw the glass across the room and smiled a little when he heard it shatter on the wood door. His mother stood next to his bed and crossed her arms, glaring down at him. He knew he was acting childish, and he didn't care. The pain had fogged his mind to the point that nothing else mattered.

It had been two days since he'd been released from the hospital, and so far, he'd only had about three hours of sleep. He knew his mother and aunt had the best intentions for him, but he couldn't stand them being around all the time, seeing him like this. So he'd acted out the only way he knew how, by throwing things and yelling at them.

He looked up from the bed he'd spent the last two days in and noticed his mother's left eye twitching, something that only happened when she was truly pissed at him.

"Dante Damiano Cardone, I'm so ashamed of you right now. You will not behave like this when Miss Rossi gets here, do you understand me?" Her voice was low and he could almost feel the vibration from it. He was saved from answering his mother, when his aunt rushed into the room.

"What's going on in here?" She moved over to his side and grabbed his hand gently. Her dark gray hair was long and flowed close around her face. She was a stout woman who held herself like she had a lot of power.

"Dante are you in much pain?" Her English wasn't very good, but she spoke it nonetheless, since his mother had set the rule many years ago that when she was in the house, they spoke English. Something even his aunt had obeyed for the last twenty-seven years. It hadn't been hard for them to follow the rule in the past, since his mother had only been in the house a few weeks out of every year. But now, she was living there full-time and he could tell his aunt was having a hard time following the rule and tolerating the other woman in her house.

Florentina Cardone was in her late fifties and the younger sister of Dante's father, Damiano, though she acted like she was the older one. She always seemed to be in charge of him, at least when his mother wasn't around.

The house Dante had grown up in was very large and had been handed down for over five generations. His father had spent his first million refurbishing his parents' small home and turning it into what it was today—a mansion. The acres of olive tree groves and vineyards spread out around the large tan, red-roofed place which sat like a beacon in the green fields of rolling hills. The view was spectacular, something he had missed while he had lived in the States over the last few years. But, since his return home he had yet to enjoy any of it.

He tried to sit up a little and was reminded of the sharp pain shooting down his left side. The pins in his leg that started just above his knee towards the outside of his thigh, and the pain in his shoulder caused such immense pain, his vision actually blurred.

He didn't blame his sister, Katie, for his injuries. After all, it had been her kidnappers that had rammed their vehicle into his own. He was just grateful that his half-brother, Ric; Ric's father, Rodrick; and Katie's new husband, Jason, had been there to help save his newly found sister from the two men, hell bent on kidnapping her.

Dante had found out the truth about his hidden half-brother, Ric, when he was in college in the States. He'd been raised to think his mother had an affair while in college and had Ric then, but just last year the truth had finally come out that his mother had been married to Ric's father and actually had two children. Ric was almost six years older than Dante. Katie, who had been raised by Rodrick Derby as his own, was in fact his full-blooded sister. Katie was almost three years younger than him.

He'd finally gotten to meet Katie for the first time at the hospital the day after his accident. He couldn't really remember meeting her that day, but she'd come back the next few days before her and her new husband had left on their honeymoon. He'd gotten to know her and Jason, quite well by the time he'd finally been released from the hospital almost two weeks later.

His mother had not only cheated his father out of a daughter, but she'd deceived them all. The entire time he had been growing up, he'd been told that her absence from the family was because her parents in the States didn't condone his parents' relationship. When the truth was, she had a completely separate family that she was spending her time with.

Growing up, he'd seen her as often as one would a distant relative. His aunt had filled the role of mother for most of his life. He could tell that now that his mother was in the house full-time, his aunt despised the fact that her brother hadn't kicked her to the curb after the truth had come out. But Damiano had been adamant about his views and feelings towards Kathleen. Shortly after Kathleen had dissolved her marriage to Rodrick, Dante's parents had officially been married.

"Dante, you need to not work yourself up so much. Here, you need to take your medicine. You drink the soup I made for you, then take these." His aunt held up the bottle of medicine he'd been ready to throw at the door after the glass.

He might be able to deny his mother, but he couldn't say no to his aunt. Looking into those dark chocolate eyes, he was reminded of his upbringing and knew he needed to obey the short woman who had raised him like her own.

"Florentina, maybe you can talk some sense into my son." His mother uncrossed her arms and walked to the doorway. "I expect him to behave when Miss Rossi gets here."

"Who is this Miss Rossi?" His aunt asked.

"Remember? She is the nurse I've hired to take care of Dante. She's a specialist in physical therapy. She's the one that's going to get him on his feet again." His mother started to walk out the door and he swore he heard her say. "Even if it kills him."

❄

Airlea Rossi was running late. Her little car sputtered and coughed up the long, muddy driveway. Her GPS told her the house was two miles ahead, but the roadway was so rugged, she didn't think her little Saab would make the trek.

Finally admitting defeat, she pulled over into the grass. Getting out of her car, she looked around and all she could see were trees and deep green, rolling fields.

Picking up her phone from her seat, she checked the GPS one more time. The little red arrow pointed in front of her, and less than two miles down the road was the blue dot that marked her destination. Tossing the phone back into her car, she stomped her foot.

"Skata!" she screamed into the field.

Just then she heard a noise and looking over her shoulder. An old, beat-up pickup truck was bumping up the lane behind her.

Waving her arms, she felt relief when the older gentleman stopped beside her car. He wore dirty overalls and had a big hat on his head.

"Hello? Are you lost?" He asked in Italian.

"Yes, I'm looking for the Cardone residence," she answered easily.

She watched as the man took off his big hat and ran his forearm across his sweaty forehead. He had a full head of very dark curly hair and was younger than she had first thought.

"What do you want at the Cardones?" He asked.

"I am the nurse hired to help with their son." She smiled.

"Well, why didn't you say this to begin with?" He put back on his hat and got out of the truck. "Your car won't make it up the drive. I'll drive you the rest of the way." He walked around the truck. "Do you have bags?"

"Yes." She felt uneasy about leaving her car in a field alongside a dirt road. Even though the car was a few years old, it didn't deserve to be deserted like this. "What shall I do?" she asked as she motioned to her car.

"Well, I can have someone come and tow it up to the main house if you want. Then we can make sure, when you leave, that we get you back down the hill safely. Usually the road isn't this bad, but we've had rain the last four days. The mud makes the road become too much for anything but the truck here to get through." He patted the truck.

Then he helped her get her two bags out of the back of her car and tossed them in the back of the truck. She rolled up her windows and locked her car, making sure to grab her purse and cell phone.

"I'm Airlea," she said holding out her hand.

"I'm Damiano Cardone." He took her smaller hand in his and shook it politely.

"Oh!" She gasped, realizing that this was her new employer. She felt her face flush with embarrassment. She'd assumed he'd been a hired hand, or just a passing farmer, not the owner of a million-dollar, world-renowned corporation.

They got into the truck and started heading up the muddy lane. She sat there and thought about how her mother had fibbed to get her this job. She couldn't blame her mother; after all, it had sounded like the deal of the century.

"Airlea, you need to get out of town for a while and regroup. This job in Italy is perfect for you. The wealth in

the Cardone family goes back for many years, and they are very well known. Their son was in a very bad accident a few weeks ago and they are looking for a nurse with your qualifications to help the boy mend, to get him back on his feet. This is what you were made to do. Plus, it pays more for a few months' worth of work than you made all last year working at the hospital."

She'd sat across from her mother, in her small apartment and chewed her bottom lip, thinking that she did need to get out of town for a while. Things had not turned out well with Angelo and since she'd lost her job, she didn't know what was left for her in Greece.

"Mama, what do I need to know about this job? How old is the boy? What are his injuries?" She'd tried to pry *information out of her mother.*

"Oh, I don't know these details," her mother had *waived her off, "you can find out when you get there. The only thing you need to know besides being a great nurse, is how to speak English. You took two years of it in school, you will be fine."*

"I almost failed two years, you mean! Did you tell them I spoke good English?" She felt like screaming.

"Yes, Airlea, you will be fine." Her mother continued *to look at the newspaper in front of her.*

So, less than two days later, she had packed up all of her belongings and left them in storage to come to Italy.

"I guess I'll be helping your son recover from his accident." She looked across the seat at Damiano.

"Yes, Dante is having a hard time recovering. I don't know how much my wife told you over the phone, but he isn't adjusting well. I think he doesn't like his medicine." He smiled over at her.

"Well, it can be tricky getting the right dosage and the right prescription. Is he in a lot of pain?" She wished he would give more details of the accident but didn't want to pry.

"I suppose so. I keep myself busy most days, since it's almost harvest time for my olive grove, but my wife, Kathleen, tells me he is being unbearable." He chuckled.

The rest of the drive was a quiet one. She didn't know what to say to the man. She desperately wished for more information. She held onto the door handle as the truck bumped up the muddy lane.

Finally, they turned a corner and she saw the house for the first time.

It was a huge half-stone, half-stucco house that sat at the top of a large hill. The grass and trees around it were well maintained, and she could just make out a large swimming pool with a pool house to the side as they pulled up.

The stone archway held a balcony that ran across the front of the house and down both sides, with ornate black iron railings. There were huge stone pillars that held up the balcony and stopped waist high on the second level. Each pillar was topped with a clay pot filled with bright red flowers. Deep, wide steps led up to the tall retreat. There were a half dozen French doors along the front and the same number along the sides, both upstairs and down.

The truck stopped in front of a large garage with six bays. Several doors were open, and she could see other well-maintained expensive cars parked inside.

"I'll just go and see about getting your car up here. You can go on in and make yourself at home. Kathleen will be somewhere around. I'll bring your bags inside." He pointed to a door, just under another balcony.

She watched him walk into the garage, she turned and looking around the yard. The last hundred feet of the drive had been done in deep red bricks and the walkway to the house had large stone steps that sat down in the well-groomed grass. Taking the pathway, she had just reached the doorway when she heard a large crash come from the open doors above her. When she heard a low rumble of cuss words, her heart skipped, knowing that someone had just fallen. Her nurse's instincts kicked in and she dropped her purse and rushed up the large, wide stairs.

She ran through the opened doors before she had time to think of what she was doing.

There, in the middle of the floor, lay the most handsome man she'd ever seen. He looked very large, sprawled out lying on his front side, and then she noticed that he was completely naked.

CHAPTER 2

*H*is left leg had the standard pins and a brace just above his knee on the outside of his thigh holding his injured bones together. His shoulder was encased in white bandages. Muscles ran down his back and her eyes followed the path to his tight butt, then traveled down his legs as she noticed the very light covering of dark hair on his arms and his legs.

She returned her eyes to his head and saw that his rich black hair was on the longer side, and it looked like he'd been running his hands through it. He wore at least a day's growth of hair on his face, which gave him a dangerous look. When she'd rushed in, he'd looked up at her with large chocolate eyes. Now he was giving her an even more dangerous look. He'd been scanning her up and down as much as she'd been looking at him.

She'd worn tan khakis and a dark burgundy button-up shirt for her long drive from the ferry which she'd taken last night to cross the sea.

"Are you all right?" She walked towards him with her hands out, ready to help him up.

"Out!" He bellowed.

"I'm here to…" She started.

"Get out!" he screamed, and she could see the veins on his neck starting to pop out as his face turned a deep red.

She took a step back. "I'm here to help you."

When he just looked at her with his eyebrows scrunched, she tried again.

"You'll need some help off the floor." She crossed her arms over her chest.

"I said," he spoke in a calm voice laced with edge, "get out, now!" She didn't move.

He was laying on a very expensive looking Persian rug, front side down so that his very tight, very gorgeous ass was up in the air. She tried to keep her eyes on his face, instead of traveling over his toned body instead.

Putting both hands on her hips, she looked down at him. "Mr. Cardone, if you care to get up off the floor by yourself ever again, just give me a call." She turned and started walking back out the open doors just as a short, gray-haired woman came running in through the inside door.

Airlea nodded her head at the woman and continued out the outside doors with her head held high. She was stopped a few feet away on the balcony by another woman. This one was younger and had rich, shoulder-length chestnut hair and wore a summer dress with yellow flowers on it. She had a warm smile on her face and her eyes twinkled with kindness.

"You must be Airlea Rossi," the woman said in English as she walked towards her, a large pile of flowers in one hand and her other stretched out for a hand shake. "I'm Kathleen Cardone."

"How do you do?" She said in English. "I'm sorry..." she motioned behind her. "I didn't mean to... um, run in, it's just that I heard a crash." Airlea struggled with finding the right English words.

"Don't worry about it, please." Kathleen smiled and motioned for her to follow her down the stairs. "I'll just go put these in some water and we'll have a quick chat in the kitchen."

Airlea followed her down the stairs, picking up her purse from where she'd dropped it earlier.

Following the woman inside, she stepped into the largest kitchen she'd ever seen. Stone pillars ran on either side of the room, and a dining area sat off to the side with a table that could easily sit a dozen people.

She stood in the doorway as the other woman walked across the tile floor, placed the flowers on the marble countertop, then started looking through the cupboards.

"They always seem to move things around," she mumbled to herself. "Oh, here it is." She pulled out a large green vase. "Well now, please come have a seat." She motioned towards the large table.

When Airlea sat at the far end, the woman walked over and took the seat next to hers.

"I've known your mother for many years. Did she happen to mention that?" She said while arranging the flowers.

Airlea shook her head, no. Her mother never mentioned the connection before.

"Well, that doesn't matter. When she called me the other day and told me about your situation, well, I knew you were perfect for the job." She stopped and smiled at her.

"My situation?" Airlea looked confused. She didn't have a situation. She was here because she'd been hired to help a boy recover from an accident. "Mrs. Cardone, before we go any farther, I feel it's my duty to mention that I don't speak very good English."

"I know. Your mother mentioned it." She waived her hand and finished arranging the flowers. "Don't worry, it won't be a problem."

"Well, I'm also used to working with children, not grown men. My mother told me your son had been in an accident, but she never mentioned that he was... full grown." Airlea felt her face turn a little pink, remembering how full grown he'd looked on the floor.

Kathleen waved her hand, as if to wave her statement off. "That doesn't matter, either. I've done my research and you're perfect to help Dante out. There is nothing that a good," she leaned forward and whispered the next words, "kick in the ass treatment couldn't help him with." She leaned back and smiled at her.

"I'm sorry?" Airlea was a little more confused.

"Airlea—I hope it's all right that I call you by your first name, please feel free to call me Kathleen—I -- understand your questions about taking on this job. Your mother and I agreed to keep certain details from you until your arrival. We thought it best to allow you time to feel more comfortable here and see what the job entailed before you made up your mind. So," she started to get up, "let me show you to your room."

"Mrs.—Kathleen," Airlea stood, "I still don't know what you expect of me."

"Well, I would think that would be clear. I expect you to babysit my son and get him out of his foul mood. To help him heal and get back on his feet. You're such a lovely girl, having you around will do one of two things."

Airlea waited.

"He will either yell and throw things at you, then try to kick you out of the house, or worse…" she said with a smile.

"Yes?" Airlea asked when Kathleen didn't finish her thought.

She laughed. "Or he'll become his charming old self and try to seduce you. Either way, it will be good for him." She smiled as she walked out the door.

Dante lay on the floor trying to get his heart rate level again. He didn't think the elevated beat had anything to do with his fall. He knew his aunt stood over him and he didn't care.

He wondered who she was. He had looked up from his fall and at first thought he had assumed she was an angel. Then she had spoken, and he'd realized she must be his new nurse, the one his mother had kept talking about. He knew he'd been rude to her and he didn't care. How could his mother hire a young nurse? And a gorgeous one at that?

She had dark caramel skin that was probably as soft as it looked. Her long, dark hair had flowed over her shoulders and had been highlighted by the sun's rays, which had come in through the open doorway behind her.

Her eyes had been the first thing that had drawn his

eyes to her face. Dark, so dark, he'd had a hard time deciphering her emotions. Maybe it was the light shining behind her, but he could have sworn she'd laughed at him. Her lips had looked just as inviting, full, plump and painted a soft hue of pink. He'd wanted to immediately storm across the room and take them with his own.

Then he'd realized he was still lying on the floor butt naked. He'd gotten mad that he'd been so vulnerable. He hated being vulnerable. So, he'd done the only thing that came naturally; he'd yelled at her. Now, looking at the floor, he realized it probably wasn't his finest moment.

"Cucciola mia, my pet, please let me help you up." His aunt walked over and placed her beefy hands under his arms and helped him back to the bed. He hated this bed. He hated this room. He wanted to go out on the balcony. He wanted a shower, not just his aunt trying to clean him with a washcloth. He hated that.

Once he was back in his bed, covered again by the blankets, he sighed and realized he was in trouble. He'd never seen a nurse that looked like that before. When his mother had told him that she'd hired a nurse to help him with his recovery, he'd pictured an old, three-hundred-pound woman with beefy hands, much like his aunt. He'd never once pictured a young woman with chestnut hair, gorgeous deep brown eyes, and lips that just called to be kissed. Not to mention a body that was straight out of the mold built for goddesses.

"What is wrong with you?" His aunt leaned over him, tucking in the blankets around him, making sure to be extra careful around his left side.

"I want a shower," he said out of the blue. Actually, he'd been headed to the bathroom when he'd miscalculated and had taken the fall that his new nurse had witnessed the aftermath of.

"I will get the bin and washcloths." His aunt started moving away.

"No, I want a shower." He pounded the bed next to him.

"But, Cucciola, it is not allowed. You will get your bandages wet." His aunt shook her head.

"I don't care. I want a shower and a shave." He moved to get up again.

"Fine, I will—" Just then his mother walked in and behind her was the goddess.

"As you can see, your room is right next to Dante's. Dante, this is Airlea Rossi. She will be taking care of you until you're back on your feet." His mother walked in and stood just inside the door.

Dante just looked at Airlea Rossi; she looked even better than he remembered. The afternoon sun was coming through his open doorway and the colors hit her face, causing it to almost illuminate the richness of her skin.

"How do you do?" she replied, looking him directly in the eyes.

He was speechless, so he just nodded his head and felt like a fool.

"Airlea, this is Florentina Cardone, my sister-in-law. Florentina helps out with Dante as much as she can. I'm afraid she is wearing herself out though."

"No, he is no problem, he has always been such a good boy." Dante half-heartedly listened to the polite conversation between the three women.

He played her name over in his head a few times—

Airlea—it sounded good in his head and he itched to say it out loud, just to see how it would feel on his tongue.

His attention snapped back to the room when he heard his aunt start talking about him wanting a shower.

"Oh, if you will give me a few minutes, I'll change and help," Airlea was saying.

The last thing he wanted this woman to do was help bathe him.

"No, I don't want your help." He knew it had come out harsher than he had intended, but he had no intentions of revealing what the sight of this woman had done to him. At least not with his mother and aunt in the room.

"Dante!" His mother crossed her arms. "You will apologize to Miss Rossi right now."

"No, Mother. You're the one that wanted me to have a nurse. I don't need anyone's help. I can shower on my own." He looked at his mother.

"Really? Is that why you were lying on the floor a few minutes ago?" Her sweet voice broke his stare and he glanced over at her again. "Because I'm sure the fall did wonders for your leg, not to mention that shoulder. You're right," Airlea said in a sharp tone, then she turned to his mother. "As you can see, Mrs. Cardone, your son is perfectly capable of helping himself. I don't know what all your worry and stress is about. We should just leave him to crawl around on the floor like a child or an animal until he decides it's time to be a man and ask for help."

Then she started walking towards the door, while Dante's mother and aunt stood with their mouths dropped open, and their eyes almost bugging out.

"Good. Go. I don't need your help," he said and smiled, thinking he had just solved his problems. Then she turned on him and marched to the end of his bed. Her eyes could have lit his mattress on fire.

"You are such an arrogant ass. Can't you see what you've done to these poor women? You've been running your aunt ragged, look at her. She looks like she hasn't had a good night's rest in weeks." She motioned toward his aunt. He did look now for the first time, and realized she was right. His aunt's shirt was untucked from her long skirt, her hair was a mess, her eyes had dark circles under them, and he could see the worry in her eyes. "And your poor mother, in the last ten minutes since my arrival, she's walked around the house like she couldn't find anything; her mind is obviously consumed with worry."

He looked toward his mother and could see it clearly in her eyes now.

"Not to mention your father. Do you know the entire drive up here; he couldn't stop talking about how great it was that you would be getting the help you needed?" She crossed her arms and took a step back. "But I can see you have everything under control now. You're right, Mr. Cardone, you don't need me, but your family certainly does. Think about that." She started walking towards the doorway and looked over her shoulder. "Oh and let me know when you want to take that shower, because something in this room stinks." Then she walked out.

He couldn't help it, he smiled as he watched her back disappear through the doorway. Then he looked at his mother's face and the smile dropped away.

"Dante Damiano Cardone, is that how I raised you?" She moved to the edge of his bed and looked down at him with disapproving eyes.

"I'm sorry, Mama." He looked over at his aunt. "Auntie, I'm sorry. I didn't know I was such a burden."

"Oh no! Cucciola mia, you are no burden to me. We don't need her." His aunt started walking towards his bed and stopped when his mother turned her head abruptly and glared at her. "Well, we don't."

"Florentina, I've hired Miss Rossi because she is a qualified nurse who has many years' experience with helping others in these circumstances. She is a practiced physical therapist." She turned on Dante now. "Which you need. So, I don't want to hear another word about her leaving this house until I say she leaves. Are we clear?" She looked at him until he nodded his agreement. Then she turned on his aunt. "This goes for you, too. Damiano agrees with me that Miss Rossi is needed, and I won't have you underfoot. You need your rest; let her take care of Dante for now." His aunt just looked at his mother. His mother took the silence as her agreement and walked out.

irlea sat down with Dante's medical file, which Kathleen had given her, in the large room which was going to be hers. Her room had a queen-sized four-poster bed, which sat in the middle of the room. She felt like the pauper in one of the old children's stories her mother used to read her.

The room was three times the size of her entire apartment. Its light mocha-colored walls made her feel welcomed. The rich cream bedspread felt soft and comfortable under her fingers. Her two bags had been sitting at the end of the bed when she'd walked in. Looking around, she wondered what she was doing here. How had she let her mother maneuver her into taking this job?

After meeting Dante Cardone, she questioned if she was going to last very long here. He might be a gorgeous package on the outside, but inside he was a spoiled brat. She'd treated him like she had all children that were having a tantrum. She was very lucky her mouth hadn't gotten her fired. Instead, Mrs. Cardone had praised how she had handled her son.

"Dante needs a firm hand. He's in a lot of pain and I know you can help him shake off this foul mood," Kathleen had told her.

What gave her the opinion Airlea was qualified to handle a twenty-something-year-old man-boy? She'd been honest and upfront with his mother: she was used to dealing with children, not men.

She knew that Dante's aunt was going to be a problem. She just knew it. After meeting the older woman, she could tell it was going to be difficult to control his recovery. She knew she had to get the upper hand with the woman right away.

Standing up, she walked over and unzipped her bag, taking out her black nurse scrubs. She started to change while thinking of her next move with Dante.

She'd looked over his medical file and knew the extent of his injuries. This gave her a good idea what he could handle and what he couldn't. Now she just needed him to trust her. And she knew he needed a shower first. But how would she manage such a feat? With children, it had been so much easier. Sure, she'd been trained to handle every situation, but she'd chosen pediatric physical therapy for a reason. She enjoyed dealing with kids more than full-grown adults.

Finally dressed, she looked at herself in the large mirror on the wide chest of drawers. Smoothing her dark hair straight, she moistened her lips and held her head up as she went to complete a task that neither she nor Dante wanted to happen.

When she walked in, he was sitting on the bed, his

arms crossed over his bare chest. He looked up and glared at her.

"I know why you're here, and you can just forget it. You are not bathing me." He spoke in English. She knew that his mother wished for everyone to speak English while she was around, so she tried to accommodate her.

"Now Mr. Cardone, you don't—" She started.

"Don't call me that," he interrupted.

Her eyebrows shot up and she gave him a questioning look. "Just what should I call you?"

"Dante would be fine." He kept his eyes glued to her face.

"Fine," she smiled, trying to show him that she, too, could be reasonable. "Now, Dante, you don't—"

"What are you wearing?" he interrupted her again.

She stopped and looked down at herself. "I'm wearing my physical therapist scrubs. Now, if you don't—"

"Why?" again he interrupted her.

She took a deep breath and closed her eyes on a wave of impatience and had a quick thought that children were easier to deal with than full-grown, sexy men. "Why what?"

"Why are you dressed like that?" He motioned to her clothes.

"I have no intention of getting my own clothes wet, and I get to keep them free of fluids such as blood, puss, vomit, and whatever else comes with my job. These are much easier to clean. Now, if you don't mind," she paused, waiting to see if he would interrupt her again. "With a little help, we can get you into the shower." She walked into the adjoining bathroom to assess how she would accomplish the task.

To her delight and relief, the bathroom was perfect for the task. Its marble floors would be slippery if they became wet, but that was the only problem she could see. The large glass shower would be easy to help him in to, and once there, there was a large bench along the stone wall of the shower for him to sit on. The shower head could easily be handed to him and he could shower himself. She walked over and set the bottle of shampoo and soap on the lower shelf, so he could reach them. Then she hung several large towels on the towel rack, within reach.

Opening the door wide, she grabbed his robe which she had found on the back of the bathroom door. Carrying it back into the room, she smiled down at him.

"Shall we get you into the shower?" He took the robe and twirled his finger in a circle. She turned around, putting her back to him while he donned the robe.

"I don't need your help. I'm only going along with this for my mother's and aunt's sakes." He said.

"I understand." She kept the smile to herself since her back was still to him. She heard him struggling to get the robe around his hurt shoulder.

"I'm done," he said, finally. When she turned around, she noticed that he had put his right arm through the sleeve, but his left one hung free since his shoulder's movement was limited. He'd tied the robe as tight as he could, and he'd moved his legs to the edge of the bed.

"How are you going to help me?" He asked.

"Well, if you'd give me your hand, I can help you stand and you can use me to lean on as you walk." She held out her hand.

"What? That's your great, medically educated plan?"

He looked shocked. "I haven't stood up in almost two weeks, I have several pins in my leg, and you expect me to just stand up and walk into the restroom with only the help of a weak, hundred-pound woman?"

"I'm not weak." She pulled him up until he stood beside her. He was a lot taller than she'd imagined and bigger. He towered over her now and she realized she just might be in trouble. Straightening her shoulders, she wrapped her arm around his waist and realized it was narrower than his chest, a lot narrower. She wrapped both her hands around him, trying to steady him as he teetered on his good leg.

"Hold still. Steady!" She tried to steady him, then they were both tumbling downward. They landed softly on the large bed. She was sprawled on top of him, her hands now trapped underneath him as his arms came around her, holding her down to him.

"Well, that worked out perfectly," he said sarcastically as he looked up at her. She could feel her face heat.

"Will you move so I can get my hands back?" She tried to push him away while pulling her arms free from underneath him. He didn't move; instead, he locked his hands behind her back and pulled her closer.

"Mmm, I don't think so. I like it right where I'm at." He almost whispered it.

She stopped wiggling long enough to look at him. "You did that on purpose!" When he just smiled, she looked into his face and could almost see red. "Mr. Cardone, you may not be aware, but you stink, and this bed and its sheets stink. And there is no doubt in my mind that it's been over a week since the last time someone tried to clean you or them. So, if you would kindly release me before I'm forced to lose my lunch all over you, we can try to remedy the stench in this stale room."

He laughed, actually laughed at her. But then he rolled to his right and then his left, releasing her arms from underneath him.

Standing up, she shook her hands to gain some blood back to them. Then she straightened her shirt and hair and looked back down at him. "Now, shall we try this again?"

After she had him settled on the shower seat still wearing his robe, she exited the room, knowing he could handle everything from there. She had warned him about getting his upper leg and shoulder too wet but knew it didn't really matter since she needed to change the bandages anyway after he showered.

She spent the next twenty minutes removing and replacing his sheets and bedding. She found several sets of sheets in a large walk-in hall closet that Kathleen had shown her during her short tour. She met Teresa, one of the workers that Kathleen had mentioned helped around the large house. Teresa was one of the two maids who worked at the house along with Rosa, who worked in the kitchen. Rosa was a frail, older looking woman who seemed friendly enough. She had been wearing an oversized apron and was busy cooking when Airlea had met her. Kathleen had said there were a dozen or so workers who worked outside with Damiano as well.

She had a short conversation with the Teresa who was very young and looked like she'd just graduated from school. She had short, dark hair and very thick glasses, which gave her a stylish bookworm look. Airlea instantly liked the girl.

She took Dante's pillows out on the balcony and

banged them together, trying to freshen them up a bit. Then she placed the new pillow cases on them and straightened his room, taking her time as she dusted his tables and nightstands off. There had been a fine layer of dust on everything, probably dirt from the fields coming in through the open doors and settling on everything.

When she was done, she knocked on the bathroom door. She heard the water shut off and then opened the door a crack. "Is everything all right?"

"Yes, I'm done." He called out.

She walked in and saw him standing in the shower, holding himself up against the wall, a towel tied loosely around his waist. She'd seen him naked earlier, but only from the back side. Now she looked at his chest and almost lost her breath. There was a little bruising left over from his accident, but for the most part, he looked healthy and whole. His chest was impressive. His dark skin stretched over the tight muscles and she could see his nipples as water dripped down him. His black hair was wet, and he'd run his fingers through it, pushing it off his face. He hadn't shaved, and the dark stubble made him look pretty damn sexy. Water dripped down his arms and legs and she had a strong urge to walk over and lick it all off of him.

Shaking her head clear, she set a pair of his slippers in front of him. "These will help with traction. We don't want you slipping and falling."

"You forgot my razor. I still need a shave." He said while he put his foot in the slippers.

"I'll bring everything to you in a while. It's almost time for dinner and for your medicine." She helped him step out of the shower.

It was complete torture when he leaned his wet, toned

body against hers as she walked him back to the room. How could a man feel so good against her skin?

She'd experienced plenty of men before and had just gotten out of a six-month relationship with Angelo. You never truly knew a person until you had to deal with them twenty-four-seven. Angelo had turned from a charming prince into a control freak who had to know her every move.

When they made it back to the room, she pulled the bed covers back farther, allowing Dante to sit on the edge. "I've laid out some clothes that I think we can manage to put on without damaging your shoulder and leg." She reached for the sweat shorts and a wide-necked t-shirt.

"I can dress myself," he barked.

"I know you can, but I need to get a look at your incisions and rods. I need to make sure everything looks clean." She bent over and grabbed the new gauze and medical tape. "If you'll sit back…" she motioned for him to lean against the headboard.

"I can change my own—" He started.

"Mr. Cardone, if you did everything yourself, what would I do? Now, sit back and please let me do my job."

He looked at her and she could see his thoughts turning. Finally, he caved and leaned back slightly. She sat on the bed next to him and started checking and cleaning his wounds.

When she was done with his shoulder, she started to pull the towel aside to work on his leg. He flinched and held the towel tight against him.

She smiled. "I think it's a little late for modesty, don't you?"

"You may think this is funny, but I don't." He growled out.

"Fine, how about we get you into the shorts first, then I can have a look at your leg." She suggested.

When he nodded, she stood and held the sweat shorts by his feet. He moved his right foot into them easily but had a harder time lifting his left leg into the hole. She bent down and held his leg up and guided it into the opening. "We'll have to work on your mobility soon." She started to pull the shorts up, but he swatted her hands aside and quickly pulled them up under the large towel and over the metal bar holding the pins. He tossed the towel aside and it landed on the floor in a wet heap. She walked over and picked it up, shaking her head.

"You would think that you'd take better care with this rug. Did you know that it's most likely a late 1800's antique Persian Kermanshah Rug? It's probably worth more than I made last year." She folded the towel and walked into the restroom to put it away.

Coming back into the room, she watched as he tried to pull his leg up onto the bed. She walked over and took it in her hands, setting it softly on the bed and placing two pillows under his knee to keep it elevated.

"Here, let me have a look at your leg now." Since he was sitting on the edge of the bed closest to the bathroom, she had to actually crawl across the wide bed to get to his left leg. He leaned his head against the headboard and closed his eyes. His arms were crossed over his bare chest since she'd forgotten to help him put on his shirt.

Taking her time, she moved his shorts up until she could remove the large, wet bandage that covered his leg. The wound was nasty looking. She could see where they'd made a small incision just above his knee, and there were four pins sticking out of his flesh which were attached to a small, metal bar.

"Is this where they had the drain?" she asked, touching the staples lightly with her fingers.

He opened his eyes and looked at her, then nodded and closed them again.

She'd forgotten her gauze on the nightstand and leaned over him to reach for it. His eyes flew open quickly. She was less than an inch from his face and he stared at her intently.

"I'm sorry, did I hurt you?" She sat back up.

He shook his head, no.

She finished cleaning and dressing the wound, wrapping the gauze tightly around his knee and thigh and making sure to cover the lower incisions where they had inserted a drain for all the fluids that built up after surgery.

"I assume you will have this bar on for around five months?" She asked.

He nodded his head again and she could swear he was trying to breathe through the pain.

She got up and stood in front of his bed, looking at him. He still had his eyes closed and his head was leaning back against the soft headboard.

"You must be exhausted. It will take a while for your strength to come back. We'll start on the therapy tomorrow. I'll bring up your dinner shortly." She turned and walked out of the room, knowing he watched her hips sway as she went out.

When she got to her room, she saw that all the dresser drawers were open, some of her clothes were on the floor, and her laptop was open. She knew that whoever had been in her room wouldn't have gotten through her password. Looking around, she didn't see that anything was missing, and she began to pick everything up and put it all away again. She wondered if one of the young maids had been looking for something to steal. She felt bad because she liked them and decided not to tell Kathleen since nothing was missing.

Florentina also watched her walk out of his room. She didn't like that the girl was here. Oh, she had promised her brother that she wouldn't raise a fuss, but seeing the attraction between the pair, she knew it was only a matter of time before Dante started acting like himself again and he tended to fall for the prettiest girl in the room. Florentina had already broken up several of his relationships in the past, this one would be no different. After all, she knew how to scare young women off.

Oh, she didn't mind him flirting with the help; after all, he was a man. What she didn't like was how the young woman had looked at him in return. She would just have to keep a close eye on them and make sure the girl didn't get the wrong idea into her head. She was the help around here and would never amount to anything more.

ante felt like he'd just run a hundred miles, and he didn't think it had anything to do with exerting himself in the shower. His damn medicine was playing havoc with his system. If he wasn't bent over in pain, he was drowning in a haze.

He was feeling a little lightheaded and knew that he had just exerted himself more in the last hour than he had in the last two weeks. How could his body betray him so quickly?

He had thought that being trapped in the hospital had been bad but being locked in this room wasn't any better. He craved getting back to work and having his normal body back. He wanted to get back to his office in the States. Hell, at this point, he'd settle for their main office in Rome.

Taking a large breath, he remembered the feeling of Airlea's fingers on his skin.

It had been pure torture not grabbing her and taking her

on his bed. His medicines were affecting him in so many ways, but they didn't seem to be getting in the way of his desires. Was she trying to kill him? She had to know what she was doing to him. The soft smell of her and the feel of her hands on his naked skin had been pure hell.

Maybe it wouldn't be such a hardship being locked in this house for a while if he had her to play with.

By the next day, he was trying his hardest to get the woman out of his house. He couldn't stand it; he couldn't stand her. Did she honestly believe he was a child? She'd walked into his room that morning and talked to him like he was ten instead of twenty-eight. His mother and aunt had been no help, either. They had just left the room and he could have sworn he saw a smile on his mother's face.

"If you don't move your butt, how can you expect to get any better?" she was saying behind his back.

He was standing for only the second time since his accident, and he wasn't happy about it. He knew it was only a matter of time before his right leg gave out. Pain was shooting up his left leg and he swore he could feel the two pins they had inserted. The blood had all pooled in his foot and he could see it starting to swell by the second. His leg was still very swollen and wrapped tightly in gauze. He'd seen the damage to his leg and knew the scar would be large. He couldn't remember much from his first few days at the hospital, but he did remember one doctor telling him he would have to walk with a cane and would probably have a limp for the rest of his life, to which Dante had replied, "The hell I will."

He was determined not to have any side effects from this whole ordeal, and he knew that Airlea was the key. He just didn't want her to know that he thought that, yet.

"You are pushing me too hard. I'm going to end up either on my ass or on top of you." He leaned a little more on her tiny frame, knowing he could have tolerated a little more, but not wanting her to see it.

"You will not; we only need to get back to your room." She shifted her weight, taking a little less of his, a sign that she knew he was not in as much trouble as he wanted her to think.

They had walked the entire length of the upstairs balcony, something he could remember doing a million times before the accident. But this time, it had seemed an impossible feat. Looking down at the length of it, he wondered why his father had to build the damn thing so big in the first place.

"See, there, we are just a few steps away." She said.

"Oh, yippee." The sarcasm rolled off his tongue and gave him little satisfaction. Finally, they reached the doors to his room. His aunt stood by his bed, a stern look was on her face.

"You are pushing him too hard." She barked.

"Mr. Cardone can handle what I've planned for him. I've looked over his medical charts and know his limits. But thank you for voicing your concerns." She said while helping him back into the room.

He watched in amusement as she dismissed his aunt with a look, something he'd never learned how to do.

She helped him walk into the restroom and shut the door behind them.

"I thought you would like to shave today." He noticed there was a chair sitting in front of the sink and mirror. His shaving items sat on a fresh towel on the counter. She helped him walk to the chair where he sat down without a word.

"I'll leave you to it." She walked, gaining more of his respect. Halfway through shaving, he heard loud voices from the next room. He tried to listen, but the thick door didn't allow much sound through.

Less than ten minutes later, Airlea walked back in the room looking a little dazed but holding her head high.

"What was that all about?" he asked before she could cross the room.

She stopped in her tracks and looked at him. "Your aunt was just voicing some of her concerns. I've managed to answer some of her questions." She continued towards him and helped him stand again.

He'd taken his time shaving and felt almost human again. He wished he could wear some normal clothes, instead of his cut-off sweats and the extra-large t-shirt. He also wished he could get back to work. So far, his mother hadn't even brought him his laptop. She had told him the first day home that he would get it when she felt he was up to working remotely, and no sooner.

He thought that she was trying to make up for all the time she'd lost raising him. She was being overly protective, more so than he was used to even with his aunt.

"I'm sorry my aunt yelled at you. She can be a little overbearing." He said.

Her perfect eyebrows shot up and she looked at him. "Oh, your aunt wasn't yelling at me. I was the one scolding her." If she hadn't been holding onto his waist, he was sure he would have fallen on his ass.

"What?" He balked.

"I've been put in charge of your health and recovery. I

don't expect anyone to interfere with my duties. Your aunt was wrong to question my authority. I was simply explaining this to her." She started moving towards the door again.

He couldn't hide his smile. How could he not respect a woman who stood up to his aunt?

Airlea was shaking. She couldn't stop, and she knew it had nothing to do with the fact that she'd been reprimanded by Dante's aunt. She could hold her own and the shaking had nothing to do with what had transpired in the next room. No, what was causing her to shake was the smile on Dante's face. Seeing it, she knew she was in trouble. His perfect, white teeth weren't the issue, nor were his yummy looking lips. It was the pure sparkle in his eyes and the deep dimples on either side of his perfect mouth that gave her stomach a little flutter and had her hands trembling.

Grabbing onto his waist again, she tried to rush him back to his bed, so she could disappear for a while and recover. After she deposited him on the side of his bed, she quickly helped him move his injured leg up to a comfortable place on top of the pillows.

"Any chance you could bring me my laptop? It's in the office, just down the hallway." He looked at her, and she saw a pleading look in his eyes.

"Yes, I'll be right back." As she started to walk out, he called out to her.

"Oh, make sure to bring the cable and the mouse sitting beside it."

Walking down the hall, she peeked into every room

until she finally found what looked like a large office. It faced the front of the house and she could see a large wood desk with the laptop sitting on it.

It took some doing, balancing the laptop, the cable, and the mouse, but she managed to get everything back down the hallway. Then she had to find a plug and ended up crawling on the floor behind his nightstand to plug it in for him. When he asked for a hard surface to use the mouse on, she handed him a book. He set it on the bed and happily went to work on his laptop.

With their work done and Dante occupied with his computer, she felt like she could take some time for herself. Lunch was an hour away and she didn't think she'd be missed if she took a brisk walk. Stopping by her room, she changed into her tennis shoes and grabbed a light sweater, since the weather called for rain later that day. She took the wide stairs past Dante's doors and walked down the rocky path past the large garage. She could hear someone banging around in there but didn't stop.

Taking a path, she'd seen earlier, she walked through the large fields towards a small cluster of olive trees. The path looked worn and she could tell it was well traveled. When she reached the first row of smaller trees, she noticed a few larger trees near the middle. She picked up a few olives that had dropped and ran them through her fingers. They were still very hard and bright green. She had heard that harvest was just a few weeks away, and she was very interested in seeing it for herself. Looking around the empty orchard, she wondered what the process was and wished she would be here long enough to witness it herself.

Dropping the olives to the soft ground, she continued her walk up the hill towards a small building. Here the ground was rockier and steeper. She enjoyed taking brisk walks and saw the climb as a challenge. She always tried to take walks back at home, even on days she was busy at the hospital. Thinking about her job caused her steps to falter. She was glad to get away from Greece. Losing her job had been a big disappointment, and knowing it was all Angelo's fault really upset her.

Stopping, she closed her eyes and took a few cleansing breaths. She didn't want to think about Angelo or the loss of her livelihood. Every time she did, her head and heart hurt. She'd cried all the tears she could over them both. She was done feeling self-pity. In her line of work, she was used to dealing with people who pitied themselves and she refused to be one of them.

Stretching her arms over her head, she looked across the field. She was halfway up to the top of the hill and could see for miles. There were a few other houses and buildings within sight, but the Cardone's place was by far the biggest building around. Its red tiled roof stood out like a beacon in the sea of green. The stone walls reminded her of an old fort she'd seen once in eastern Greece as a child.

Damiano and Kathleen Cardone were nothing like the people she'd heard about on the news. She'd heard the whole story about what had transpired last year. She'd even had the pleasure of meeting their daughter, Dante's sister Katie, earlier last month. Of course, she hadn't known it was Katie Derby at the time or that Katie had a sexy older brother. She'd only seen a woman in trouble and in love.

She'd been impressed with the man, Jason, who had

carried the unconscious Katie into the hospital. She'd enjoyed talking to Katie later that evening as she'd made her rounds. She'd purposely changed shifts, so she could see how the couple was getting along. The man had a nasty concussion and had slept for most of the night. Katie, however, had sat up and talked to Airlea for a few hours.

Airlea had enjoyed learning more English from Katie and had even helped her out with her Greek and Italian.

She was almost to the top of the hill when she heard a noise behind her. Looking back down the path, she saw an old border collie jogging up the path towards her. She looked around to see if anyone else was around. Seeing no-one, she called to the dog with a friendly voice.

"Hello, are you a nice dog?" Upon hearing her voice, the dog's tail started wagging quickly. Smiling, she knew she'd received her answer.

When the dog arrived by her side, she bent and let it sniff her hand. When it sat and held up its paw, she laughed and shook it.

"Well, hello." She looked at the dog's collar and saw that her name was Lucy. She chuckled at the human name. The black and white dog just looked at her with what could only be described as a smile on her doggie lips. "Well, I was going to walk up to that shed and back down. Are you up for the walk?"

The dog barked at her and got up, its tail wagging, so Airlea continued up the pathway with Lucy following close behind her.

She could get used to living in the country. She'd grown up just outside of Venice in the small town of Adria, and after finishing school, she'd rushed to the city for medical training in Rome. She'd enjoyed living in downtown Rome in the small dorms on campus. She'd made friends and had quickly decided that she wanted to pursue physical therapy instead of being an ER nurse like her mother.

When she made it to the small building, she took a deep breath and looked around. From here she could see down another valley, at the bottom of which was a large lake surrounded by small trees. She made a mental note to make that trek in the near future. She sat down on a large rock and Lucy sat next to her, putting her head on Airlea's lap. She pet the dog and thought about her future.

Maybe losing her job had been a blessing in disguise. She'd been thinking in the last few months about getting back to Italy again. Maybe she'd find a little town and open her own therapy clinic somewhere.

She had quite a bit in savings. It wasn't enough to do anything elaborate, but if her mother would help out, she might have enough to start off. She could always see about getting a loan at the bank, but she didn't really like being in debt. She'd paid off her student loans in the first year of working at the hospital. She'd sacrificed a lot that year to pay everything off. Meals, friendships, and even dating had all been put on the back burner.

Thinking about dating only brought her mind back to Angelo. After him, she had no intention of dating anyone in the near future. After being burned by him, she didn't think she would be able to easily trust again. After all, he had been able to hide who he really was from everyone he'd worked with for years at the hospital. Everyone there had assured her that he was the nicest man, so she'd taken a chance and gone out with him after he'd asked her a dozen or so times. Everything had worked out great that first six months. He'd really seemed like the nice guy everyone had talked about. It wasn't until after he'd moved in that he'd started to show his true colors.

Controlling didn't describe it well enough. He'd ruined her. That sounded harsh, but in fact, she no longer felt like she ever wanted to get married. She couldn't believe that at one point, she'd thought he was the right man to marry, and he'd turned out to be the worst mistake of her life.

She didn't need or want a man in her life right now, but that didn't mean she couldn't enjoy herself. She'd always been open with herself about her desires, taking her pleasures where she found them, and Dante Cardone was very easy on the eyes. Even though he'd been rude to her, she knew it was probably only his pain talking. No one could be that rude all the time, at least she hoped not. Breaking him into the routine she'd need him on was going to be a challenge. She hated being one of those strict physical therapists, but she needed him on his feet more often than he was. With an injury like his, blood circulation was vital at this stage. She needed to assess if he had any nerve damage in his shoulder and leg.

Just then Lucy stood up and started walking back down the path. Taking the hint that it was time to go, she got up, dusted off her scrubs and started down the narrow pathway.

Dante watched Airlea walk down the path with Lucy. He

could just see the pathway if he leaned to the other side of his bed. When he'd seen her go by his doors half an hour earlier, he'd set his laptop down and watched her walk up the hill. Why he did this was still a mystery to him. He knew he had felt an instant pull of attraction towards her. After all, he wasn't blind. Why was a woman like her doing a job like this?

If he knew his mother, he didn't doubt she'd hired her just to help her friend out, like she'd said. His mother was a meddler. Even though he hadn't gotten to spend a lot of time with her growing up, he'd learned that lesson early on. It had almost crushed him when he'd found out about his mother's other life. He'd known for a few years that she had another son in the States. She'd always maintained that he was from an earlier relationship in her college years. But almost four years ago, he'd discovered the truth about his half-brother Ric Derby.

Finding out about Katie Derby, his full blood sister had been the real shocker. He looked over at the dresser and saw the picture his mother had framed and set there. It was impossible not to see the blood connection between the two faces. His face was still pale from surgery and his eyes were clouded with drugs. The picture of them at the hospital a few weeks ago was a good reminder for him of what she looked like since the drugs had dulled his memory.

His sister was beautiful and well worth the pain he was now going through. He would easily do what he had done again if her life was in jeopardy again. He'd always wanted a sister or brother. He'd been one of those kids that had constantly asked his mom for one when she'd been around. Now he knew why she'd always looked at him the way she had; she'd felt guilty for keeping his sister from him.

Since his return to Rome, he'd tried to stay clear of his mother, but after his surgery, it became harder and harder. His father had insisted that he recover here, at his childhood home just outside of Rome, and of course, his mother had been living their full time since they had married almost a year ago.

Instantly she'd felt it necessary to try and coddle him, so he'd made a point to not allow it by throwing things while she was around. He found it quite therapeutic hearing the crashes and watching her clean up the mess. After all, she hadn't been there most of his life.

Looking up at his door, he watched his aunt walk in with a tray of food.

"She works you too hard," his aunt said, setting down the tray on his nightstand. "I don't like it, or her. I can take care of you. After all, I've been doing it all your life while she was out—"

"Don't," he looked up at her, "you know better than to bring up the subject of my mother."

He'd seen the concern in his aunt's eyes earlier when he'd been walking on the patio. To be honest, it had been refreshing to be outside and upright. He'd had enough of beds and the indoors for a while. What he really wished for was to take a long walk like Airlea had. Looking down at his leg, he started getting frustrated.

He'd always been in great shape, and ever since childhood, he'd been very active. Futbol was his sport. He loved the large open field, the ball to kick around, his friends, and the challenges. He'd actually been so good during his college days in the US that he'd tried out for a professional team, only to be shot down. He'd been upset for a few weeks, but then after he'd learned about his brother, he had rushed to Portland to take over his father's business, New Edges. He'd been too curious not to get closer to the man, to see him and learn all he could about Ric. He supposed it was for the best. He was a businessman, not a futbol star.

He still kept in shape by running and playing the occasional game with friends, but looking at his leg now, he doubted futbol was in his future. Damn, he hated being weak. It made him into someone he didn't like being.

His aunt was giving him a look he knew all too well. It was the look she gave him when she was trying to make him feel guilty about something.

"Listen," he said as his aunt sat down beside him on the bed, "I know you can take care of me, probably better than most, but the nurse is here to appease my parents. If mom says the woman stays, then I suppose we will just have to put up with her for now. I don't like it any better than you do."

Just as those last words slipped from his lips, Airlea walked through the door, her head held high and determination in her eyes.

"Well, now that it's all settled that no one wants me around, it's time for your lunch, medication, and rest. Miss Cardone, if you'd be so kind as to shut the door on your way out, thank you."

Airlea didn't even stop to allow his aunt to say anything in reply. Instead, she walked over and took his laptop from his lap and set it on the dresser. She took the tray from his nightstand and placed it across his lap. Then she stood and watched his aunt leave the room with a huff. He watched with humor as his aunt gave her a more viscous stare than he'd ever seen from her before, as she closed the door with a slight click.

"You shouldn't talk to my aunt in that tone. She's done so much for me. She's practically my mother." He said, settling the tray across his lap.

"I understand you're having a hard time with me being here. If we could just all agree that no one wants me here and move on, maybe we can have you walking on your own in record time. Until then, I am in charge of what takes place with your schedule, is that understood? Now, eat while I go get your medication." She walked into the restroom.

He couldn't stop it; the glass was in his hand, and before he knew what he was doing, it was flying across the room and shattering against the bathroom door she'd just walked through.

She leaned out the door and looked at him with her eyebrows raised.

"I'm in charge of my own damned self. I don't know who you think you are, but I didn't ask for you to be here. I didn't ask for your help and if I want my aunt to take care of me, then I better not hear another word about it." He was losing steam. The morning walk had taken a lot out of him, but he was damned if he'd show the bossy nurse that he was tired.

"Feel better?" Upon her half smile, he started to pick up his plate.

"If you throw that, you won't have any lunch. I will personally see to it that you don't get anything else to eat until dinner." She turned and walked back into the bathroom without another word.

He thought about it, then set the plate back down on the tray. Damn. He was just too hungry to chance it. What was happening to him? He couldn't seem to control his moods anymore. Maybe it was the medication they had him on that made him feel like a hormonal teenage girl. He'd never had any ups and downs before. He'd been a steady, in-control kind of guy his entire life. Even when his mother had betrayed his father and lied to him his whole life, he'd taken it with dignity.

Now he couldn't even control his temper around one of the sexiest women he's ever seen. Maybe it was her and not him? Yeah, that was it. Hell, he knew he was trying to fool himself into believing it was someone else's fault. The truth was the pain and being cooped up had done something to him. Maybe he needed to see a shrink?

Just then she walked back into the room from the bathroom. She stopped and looked down at him. He hadn't eaten anything yet; he was just staring at his plate like it was full of foreign objects.

"It's not you, you know." She walked over and handed him two large pills.

He looked up at her and raised his eyebrows to show that he didn't know what she was talking about.

"The mood swings. They come with the lack of energy and all the pain. You'll find a steady balance in the next few days. Until then, just know that if you ever do actually hit me with something, I won't hesitate to throw something right back at you." She smiled at him and for the first time in almost two weeks, he laughed.

"If I do actually hit you, feel free to hit me back. I have a terrible throwing arm." He smiled.

She smiled back. "I have perfect aim. Go ahead, eat your lunch. I'll just take your laptop and…"

"No, don't. It's the first time in weeks I've been allowed to get on the thing. I have over a thousand emails I need to read." He wasn't opposed to begging. She looked at him and he hoped she would take pity on him.

"Fine, but you need your rest. I'll come back and check on you in an hour. Now take your medicine." She waited as he willingly swallowed the pills, knowing that the pain he was feeling would soon be dulled.

"I'll be back in an hour. Enjoy your lunch." She started to leave.

"Airlea?" He called out.

She stopped at the door and looked over her shoulder at him. "Yes?"

"Thanks." He felt like a child sitting in his bed, the food tray balanced on his lap.

Instead of replying, she just smiled and walked out. He wished she hadn't heard or seen his tantrum earlier. Damn, he was going to have to try to control his moods better with her around.

Maybe he just needed something else to keep his mind off his pain. When she was around he was either annoyed at her or aroused by her. Maybe it was time to explore the other side since annoyance was just earning him more broken dishes.

Airlea had made it a pattern to take walks with Lucy every

day. She would take the olive grove path or another shorter path that lead over the rolling hills past a large field of grapes.

It was three days since Dante had thrown the glass at her and his moods were in full swing. Just yesterday as they were walking on the balcony, he'd actually sat down on the ground, refusing to walk any further. He'd been doing so well, and she had been thinking it was almost time to try teaching him to go down the stairs.

Then his aunt had walked out on the balcony and persisted he rest. She just couldn't get the woman out of her hair. She questioned everything Airlea did and tried to take over with his physical therapy. Now, to top it off, she had purposely gone against Airlea's strict orders. Airlea was trying to cut back on Dante's pain medications, as she felt he didn't need to be taking so many. A lot of patients start relying too heavily on them and knowing one's limits for pain was always key in stopping the dependency before it began. She didn't want Dante to become too reliant on them. She had talked it over with everyone, and they had all agreed to cut back. Apparently, his aunt had only gone along with her plan for show.

A few days later, she was on her way back to the house from one of her walks one afternoon when Damiano stopped her. He was working inside the garage on an older car.

"How's my son doing?" He asked.

She walked over to look at the car and stood next to him. "Dante is doing fine. I think we will try to conquer the stairs tomorrow. I've talked to your wife about getting him some crutches when you take him to get his staples removed. She said she would. She sounded excited to see him back on his feet."

"I know we were really worried about him being able to walk. The doctor said he'd walk with a limp and..." Damiano chuckled and she noticed for the first time how much Dante took after his father. "He told the doctor to go to hell and that he wouldn't walk with a limp. Do you know? He actually bet the man money that he wouldn't."

She laughed. It sounded like something he would do. In the last few days, she'd learned more and more about Dante. His medicine and the fact that he was injured played a lot on his emotions. She could tell he felt helpless for the first time in his life. Some people could handle being helped, others didn't like showing weakness. Dante was definitely in the latter category.

"Well, I hope he isn't too much trouble for you. I know he's been acting up, but I assure you, he's never acted that way before. He was always a very good child. A little strong headed, but he's never been mean before." He shook his head.

"You did a fine job raising him. I'm a pretty good judge of character, especially when it comes to my patients, and I can tell it's just the medicine and injury causing his problems now." She patted his arm.

Damiano smiled at her. "You're a good girl. I knew your mama. She's the one that introduced me to Kathleen. Did she ever tell you that?"

Airlea shook her head, no.

Damiano laughed. "Someday, maybe your mother will tell you the story."

She'd left Damiano working in the garage as the sun

slipped below the hills and walked up the stairs into Dante's room.

She stopped at the door when she saw him lying half on the bed and half off. Something wasn't right. Rushing to his side, she tried to get him back on the bed and when he didn't move, she panicked. Shaking him hard, she looked for any sign of life. When he didn't even flinch, she reached up with shaky hands to take his pulse.

CHAPTER 5

*A*irlea rushed down the large staircase in the entry hall to confront the person she knew was the cause of Dante's condition. When she entered the large room, she saw that Kathleen, the cook, and two maids were helping to clean away the dishes from the earlier dinner. Trying to calm herself down before what she knew would be a huge confrontation, she took three deep breaths to relax.

She wasn't afraid of confrontation, but she'd always chosen to avoid them when possible. Seeing Dante lying on the bed, too weak from the pain pills to even lift his eyelids, had angered her. He'd been making great physical progress in the last few days. His moods were still bad enough that earlier that afternoon he'd thrown a whole tray across the room, shattering the picture of him and his sister on the dresser. Then he'd yelled for her to get out so loudly she'd heard the windows vibrate.

When she'd found him drugged, laying on the bed almost unresponsive, she'd rushed to the restroom and counted his medication. Seeing that four pills were missing, she knew immediately who'd given them to him. She'd not only gone against Airlea's wishes about cutting back on his medicine, she'd actually doubled his last dose.

There was only one thing she could do besides confronting the woman, but Airlea didn't think that going behind her back to her brother was the adult choice. At least it wasn't her first choice for correcting the issue. If this didn't work, though, she wasn't opposed to tattling on Florentina.

Seeing the woman washing dishes in the kitchen, she nodded her head towards Kathleen who was cleaning the stove, stirring something that smelled like jelly.

"Florentina, may I have a word with you?" She asked.

"I'm in the middle of cleaning. You can wait." The woman didn't even look up from her task.

"No, this can't wait. Did you give Dante his medication tonight without my permission?" She held her ground.

"He was in pain." She didn't even pause as she rinsed a large pan with strong, fast strokes. "His nurse was neglecting him, so I gave it to him."

"Do you remember me telling everyone yesterday that I was cutting back on his medication?" She stared at the woman's back, knowing that she had the full attention of everyone in the room at that moment.

"Yes, I don't agree. He was in pain." She pulled the pan over to the drying rack.

"Airlea, what's this all about?" Kathleen asked. "Is Dante in more pain?"

"No, Kathleen, we are lucky that Dante isn't in a coma." Airlea turned on Florentina, "You gave him twice his normal dose of pain pills. That amount, given regularly, can kill a man."

Florentina almost dropped the knife she was cleaning. "What? What have you done?"

"Me?" Airlea asked. Florentina was looking towards Kathleen with concern in her eyes.

"I told you this young girl would be the death of our boy. She is too young to know what she is doing. How could you let her into our home to take care of our boy?" Then the older woman turned on Airlea and pointed the knife in her direction. "If you have harmed him, I will kill you." She dropped the knife in the sink and rushed from the room.

"Kathleen—"Airlea started.

"Don't! You don't have to explain. I'm not deaf. I heard Florentina own up to giving him the pills. Is Dante going to be all right?" Kathleen's eyes were full of concern.

Airlea nodded her head.

"Good. Florentina is a meddler, she has always been." She walked over and pulled open a large drawer. Then she turned and handed Airlea a small silver key. Airlea could see anger and concern on Kathleen's face. "Here, this is the key to the top drawer in Dante's bathroom. Lock the medicine in there and keep the key with you at all times. Please, don't let that woman upset you. God knows I've had years of dealing with her and ignoring her is the path I've chosen."

Airlea took the key and looked at Kathleen. "Thank you. Dante may sleep for two whole days, but he'll be fine. This little stunt has set him back though. He was starting to control his moods, but this afternoon, after she must have given him the pills…" She shook her head. "Well, let's just say it will take a while for him to adjust again. Fentanyl is not a drug you want to mess with. It's highly addictive and causes so many side effects. That's why I was cutting him back to half the dose his doctor recommended. Plus, he can handle the pain. I can see it. Thanks for the key and for believing in me."

"Airlea," Kathleen smiled and patted her hand. "I trust you completely."

When Airlea walked back into Dante's room, Florentina was leaning over him, shaking him.

"I've checked his vitals, and he's fine. He's just asleep. It will take around twenty-four hours for the drug to get out of his system. I'll need to watch him all through the night."

"No! I will sit with him." The woman stood and crossed her arms over her chest.

"Haven't you done enough damage this evening?" Airlea stood her ground as the woman rushed to stand right in front of her.

"Mark my words. If any harm comes to this boy, I won't hesitate to ruin you." She growled out.

Airlea walked past her and into the restroom without replying. She dumped the pill bottles in the top drawer and locked it, placing the key on the chain around her neck, next to her Saint Raphael medallion.

When she entered the room again, Florentina was gone. She knew she was in for a long night but watching Dante's vitals every hour was imperative. She remembered her worry when she'd walked in and found him unresponsive. Shivering, she tried not to think about it. She realized she was shaking from the confrontation with his aunt. The woman just wasn't right. Something was off and Airlea seemed to be the only one to see it.

Walking over to the large open doors, she shut them on a cool night breeze. The weatherman had called for rain and it was already starting; she'd even seen a few bolts of lightning in the sky. To prepare for the long night ahead of her, she went to her room to switch into more comfortable clothes.

It wouldn't be the first time she'd sat up all night with a patient. Usually, they were small children crying for a parent that couldn't be there, and she'd been the only comfort they'd had. But staying up and checking someone's vitals every hour usually wore you and the patient out. That was if the patient was responsive.

In her room, she changed into a light pair of silver sweats and a white tank top then threw a large green sweatshirt over it all. Grabbing one of the books she was reading, she took her throw blanket with her and was ready to settle down for a night of watching Dante.

Dante couldn't wake up from the bad dream. He knew it was a dream because Velociraptors didn't really exist but remembering that little bit of knowledge didn't stop him from running as he was being chased by four of the large carnivores. Of course, as all dreams go, everything and everyone was determined to stop his escape from the giant beasts. His body wouldn't work correctly. His left leg was hard for him to control, slowing him down. He'd just made it to the bunker in the middle of a large field where, in his dream state, he knew there was safety when he felt cool fingers on his forehead and was shaken from the dream.

"Dante are you alright?" A silky, sexy voice said from above him.

Cracking his eyes open, he saw the most beautiful woman he'd ever seen. Her dark hair fell over her shoulder in a loose braid and he wondered if it was as soft as it looked. Her large sweatshirt fell off one shoulder to expose the soft skin underneath and a thin, white strip of an undershirt. Her dark eyes showed concern. She was biting her lips in worry and he wondered if those were as soft as they looked, too.

"Who?" He tried to clear his mind, "Who are you?" he asked as he reached up and ran the braid through his fingers. It was as soft as it looked, then he pulled her head down to his to test her softness and taste.

Her hands came up to his chest and she tried to pull away from him, at least until their lips met. He felt the shock from her mouth on his zip through his body and all of a sudden everything was clearer. This was Airlea, his nurse. He was in his parents' house near Rome, recovering from an accident.

Then her tongue darted out to lick his lips and his mind fogged up again. Her hands were in his hair, then running over his bare chest and arms. He wrapped his arms around her, holding her closer, never wanting to let go.

She tasted like cherries, sweet and tart at the same time. He enjoyed her mouth as she nibbled on his lips, and he closed his eyes on a moan as she ran that mouth down his neck and licked her way to his chest.

He must be dreaming still. This time, he didn't want to wake up. For the first time in weeks, he felt himself stir and wanted to bury himself in her. He wanted to flip her over and take her, quickly. When he started to move to do just that, the pain was instant. It shot up from his leg and came down from his shoulder.

She noticed his flinch and pulled back. He watched her eyes and could see the moment when she realized what she'd done, what they'd done.

"Oh, I'm sorry. Are you hurting?" She pulled his covers aside, looking at his bandages. There was no hiding the fact that he'd been aroused, his boxers tented over his erection. He tried to pull the sheet back over him, but she just slapped his hand aside.

"Stop." She was focused on his bandages, paying no attention to his mighty erection, which only made him question if it was indeed mighty in her eyes. "Damn! You're bleeding."

That got his mind off his erection. He looked down and he could see the deep stain of blood on his white bandages.

"Damn." This time it was him who cussed. "I haven't done that since the hospital. Is that bad?"

"Most likely not. I'll just take a look. Let me go get some fresh bandages." She got up and left the room.

He watched her leave and realized he liked seeing her walk away in the tight sweatpants she wore. He couldn't see a panty line and wondered if she had any on underneath the light cotton.

Shaking his head clear, he wondered why he couldn't seem to stay focused. Here he was getting blood all over his mother's linens and all he could think about was getting his nurse between those very sheets.

"It's probably another side effect from the overdose." She said, frowning.

"What? What overdose?" He tried to sit up a little, to give her better access to his leg.

Her head was bent over him as she gently removed his soiled bandages. "Your aunt gave you too many pills."

He thought about it, then he said. "No, she didn't."

The first thing Airlea thought of was that she had falsely accused a woman of overdosing her nephew. Her hands shook as she cleaned the small tear at his incision point.

"She didn't give you four pills to swallow the other afternoon?" She asked, trying to keep her voice calm.

"No, she gave me two, and then she had me drink it all down with warm tea that tasted like it had gone bad." He cringed.

Airlea's mind sharpened and she realized that his aunt had drugged his tea. "She must have put the other two pills in your tea. Dante, you've had a double dose of Fentanyl. I've been checking on you every hour for the last two days. This is the first time you've actually been coherent."

"Two days? I've been asleep for two days?" He blinked a few times, looking at her.

"Yes, you really had us all worried. I haven't seen your aunt since that night. I guess she left the house. Your mother and father have been in and out during the day, checking on you." She cleaned the small cut area and put some antibiotic salve over his incision. "We should have been more careful. I guess it could have been a lot worse. Your staples don't come out for a few more days, and your pins and wireframes still have a few months before they can be removed. It looks like we just pulled out one a little early."

She tried to smile up at him and avoided looking at him directly in the eyes. How could she have let herself get carried away like that? She'd all but jumped him. She might as well have just grabbed a pair of pliers and remove all his staples herself. She'd crossed that professional line with him and now there was an uncomfortable silence in the room.

She focused on her task of re-bandaging his incision area. "When you go into the doctor, they'll probably take a few x-rays and update you on what you can do, physically. Then we can start with the next phase of your therapy. We need to get your leg moving more for good blood flow."

"Why did you think that I had been overdosed?" He asked, looking at her.

She looked up at him. His eyes were clear for the first time in days and she could see that he was trying very hard to concentrate on what was going on.

"You've been in a drug-induced state for two days. Do you remember taking that picture?" She pointed to the photo that sat on the dresser of him and his sister.

"No, I'm told it was the day after my surgery." He frowned.

She nodded her head, "They had you on some very strong medication at the hospital. I know you don't remember much. The last few days you've had a low heart rate and low blood pressure, and you were drowsy and anxious. Your breathing was slowed to almost non-exis-tent. Plus, just look." She pointed to the new bandage. "Bruising and bleeding is a side effect of an overdose of Fentanyl. There is no reason you should have bled that much from just popping one of your staples. And look at the new bruises forming here." She ran her hand lightly over his shoulder. "Dante, you were given a very high dose of medicine. Too high."

He seemed to take it all in, to be thinking about things. "Where is my aunt?"

"We don't know. She left shortly after admitting she gave you the medication. I don't think she knew what could happen. I didn't get a chance to explain…"

He took her hand and she looked up into his dark eyes. His hair needed to be cut and he needed another shave. His chocolate eyes were clear, though, and she realized he looked wonderful.

"What time is it?" He ran his hand over his face.

Shaking her head clear, she looked at the alarm clock. "Seven."

"Morning or night? I can't tell. Is that the sunrise or sunset?"

She smiled. "Sunrise."

"Give me a phone." He sat up a little more.

irlea sat at the kitchen table and watched Florentina cry into her brother's shoulder. Dante had called her, and she'd immediately arrived back home, her face puffy and red from crying. She actually looked thinner and frailer somehow. Airlea started to feel bad.

"Damiano, I'm so sorry. I didn't know what the drug would do. I just wanted to help, he was in so much pain." She said between sobs.

"I know, Florentina." Damiano patted her.

Then Airlea watched as Florentina glared at her over her brother's shoulder, which caused a shiver to run down her spine. She'd thought the woman was just an overly protective aunt, but that look told Airlea more about the woman than anything else had so far. The remorse she had been feeling a few seconds ago was gone, and in its place was a desire to protect Dante and herself.

A few hours later as she was waiting for Dante to finish showering, she had pulled all his dirty sheets off his bed and was searching the walk-in closet for more clean sheets. When she heard a noise behind her, she spun around to find Florentina quietly closing the door as she stepped into the small space.

"I know you don't understand how things work around here, so I'll clue you in. You are to stay away from Dante in a personal matter. Do you understand?" Florentina had backed her into the corner. Instead of retreating and bumping her back against the shelves that lined the back wall, Airlea stood her ground.

"I have never gotten involved with a patient before." She said in a calm voice.

"Yes, but I've heard you worked with children until now. Dante is no child. You will stay clear of him or you will answer to me." She shook her finger in front of her face.

Airlea pulled her chin up higher and looked the woman in the eyes. The nerve of this woman, cornering her in a closet to tell her this. Then her mind flashed to earlier that morning and the kiss she'd shared with Dante. She couldn't fool herself into thinking she hadn't been affected by his hot mouth on hers, or the way his hands had lit small fires on her exposed flesh. She kept trying to tell herself all day that it had been the drugs in his system that had caused the incident. But she had been dreaming about kissing him since her arrival, and espe-cially while she had watched him sleeping the last two days. How could she not stare at him and notice that his mouth was made for kissing, that his chest and arms were powerful? She fought the urge to run her hands up and down him, playing with the muscles that corded along the lines.

"I never get emotionally involved with patients." She

looked at the older woman and felt that her point couldn't be clearer.

The woman nodded her head but didn't back away.

"If you ever make me look bad in front of my family again, I will do everything in my power to destroy you." Then she turned and walked out of the closet without another word.

It took Airlea a few minutes for her hands to stop shaking. She wasn't afraid of Florentina, she was madder than anything. She knew there was no way that Florentina could have witnessed their kiss that morning. After all, she'd been MIA for two whole days and had only returned after Dante had called her and begged her to come back.

The scene in the kitchen had been repeated between Florentina and Dante earlier. He'd hugged her and forgiven her all while big fat tears slid down the older woman's face.

Something just wasn't right about Florentina. Airlea liked to think she was an excellent judge of character. After all, in her line of work she'd witnessed so many people change right before her eyes. She'd watched mean people turn into kinder characters and the kindest, soft-spoken person become a raving lunatic. She knew that pain and vulnerability tended to change people's personalities.

But then she thought about Angelo. She'd misjudged him from the first time she'd met him. It had even taken a few years of knowing him before she finally went out with him. Thinking about it, maybe subconsciously she'd known there was something hiding deeper within him.

Mentally shaking herself from the memory of Angelo, she grabbed the pile of linens and walked out of the closet and back to Dante's room. As she made the bed, she tried not to think about how nice it had felt to be pulled down in this very bed and kissed until her toes had wanted to curl. He had needed a shave and she could still feel her chin tingle from his scratchy face, which had felt like heaven on hers.

Trying to think about something else, she remembered the scene his aunt had made earlier. She couldn't blame Dante for forgiving her. She'd been very close to her own aunt when she'd been alive. She had spent every summer at her place in Venice when she had been a child. Her cousins had been like the siblings she'd always wanted. Anthony and Gilbert were quite a few years younger than her and she'd doted on them like they were her own. Actually, they were the reason she had decided to work with children. She'd been such a natural when dealing with the two boys that her aunt had decided to have her stay every summer until she'd gone away to college. She had only lived two hours from them but spending the whole summer in Venice made her feel like she was such an adult.

Just as she finished making the bed she heard the water turn off in the bathroom. Knowing he would need help, she knocked on the door and went to help him get out of the shower.

Not giving Florentina another thought for the rest of the evening was easy, since she stayed busy with Dante. Since waking up, he'd been demanding to walk around. He was probably feeling the effects of not moving a muscle for two days, and no doubt was sore from just lying there. She'd tried to move his good leg around while he'd been out, but every time she'd tried, he'd almost kicked her, so she'd given up.

She walked into the bathroom and seeing him wet and

wrapped in nothing, but a towel affected her. His hair needed a trim and he needed another shave.

"Do you want to shave?" She asked.

When he nodded his head in reply, she realized he was avoiding making eye contact with her.

"You don't have to apologize for kissing me." She smiled and noticed that his eyes had zeroed in on hers.

"I wasn't going to." He growled it out.

She tilted her head and tried another tactic. "Why not?"

He was standing just outside the shower now, holding onto the towel rack and looking at her. He was blushing like a schoolboy, which only made her smile even more.

"You are so easy to tease." She walked over and grabbed his arm and helped him hobble over to the chair that sat in front of the mirror. He leaned on her for support and had yet to touch his bad leg to the ground. She knew he needed to move it around and not put too much pressure on it. He'd yet to use the cane that sat leaning against the wall. Every time she tried to hand it to him, he would toss it on the floor and scowl at it.

He sat down quietly and avoided looking at her. She stepped back and leaned against the door.

He started putting shaving cream in his hand, but when he noticed she wasn't leaving the room, he turned and looked at her and asked. "Are you going to stand there and watch me?"

"I was thinking about it. I've never witnessed a man shaving before." She said.

His eyebrows shot up. "Surely you've dated before."

"Oh yes, but I haven't seen any of them shave before. My father died when I was very young, and I was raised by my mother and aunt for the most part."

"I'm sorry, it must have been hard on you." He continued to look at her.

"No, not really. I knew he loved me and my mother and aunt never hesitated to show me their love. I had a good childhood. How about you?" She watched him. He was now spreading the shaving cream on his face and stopped to look at her in the mirror.

"I had an interesting childhood. I, too, was raised by a parent and their sibling. My father and aunt were here one hundred percent of the time, as my mother came and went." He dropped his eyes and focused on his task.

She watched him glide the razor over his face and marveled at his smooth strokes, which only got her thinking about his hands and how they would feel on her. She'd had a few lovers in her life and she didn't feel guilt or regret about any of them, except for her last one. Regret wasn't really the right word for what she felt about him; dread was more like it. She tried to block away those memories of her time with Angelo, like a bad movie that you wanted to forget spending a bundle to see and wasting all that time watching.

Her eyes watched Dante's hands and remembered how he'd pulled her down on top of him. She'd felt every inch of him and had wanted to dive under the covers and enjoy herself. She remembered what his mother had said the day she'd arrived. She even understood that sex was a natural step and if he was focused on her, he couldn't be focused on self-pity, the phase of recovery that most patients ended up being stuck in the longest.

Sex with Dante would not only be fun, it might help her heal from the betrayal she'd suffered. Recovery from a relationship was not much different than recovering from an accident. You just needed a little time to get back on your feet, but once there, you had to keep moving to get the juices flowing. And boy, could Dante make her juices flow. Since arriving she'd had several dreams involving him, each one steamier and more detailed than the last.

She was so deep in her thoughts she didn't register that he had finished his task and was staring at her in the mirror.

"I didn't apologize, because I want to do it again." He said, his eyes roaming over her.

She watched him in the mirror and knew that he could tell what she'd been thinking about. Walking slowly over to him she stopped and leaned against the counter-top, looking down at him.

"Your aunt warned me to stay away from you and your mother said…" she chuckled.

"What did my mother say?" He looked up at her.

"That you'd either throw things at me or try to seduce me." She smiled.

"My aunt can go to hell and my mother was wrong." He frowned a little.

"Oh?" Her eyebrows shot up.

"I'm not trying to seduce you. It's you who has seduced me. You hold all the power here, Airlea." He reached up and touched a lock of her hair that had fallen forward.

Liking the sound of that, she smiled. She was shocked when he placed both of his hands on the counter-top on either side of her and pulled himself up. Keeping his hands on the counter, he leaned in and took her mouth in a soft kiss. She reached up and ran her fingers over his freshly shaved face. It was smooth, and she enjoyed the feel of it in her hands and on her face as he nibbled on her bottom lip. She moaned and held onto his good shoulder lightly for support, enjoying the fresh smell of his shaving cream and aftershave. She knew he was balancing himself on his good leg and didn't want him to feel any discomfort that might stop him from continuing to kiss her.

Running her tongue across his bottom lip, she nipped at it playfully and then kissed it all better. His hands were still on the counter-top, helping him stay upright. She wished they were running over her and wondered how they would feel on her heated skin.

Pulling back a little she tried to act light and friendly, but she couldn't deny she'd been affected to her core.

"You know; you're going to seriously piss off your aunt if you keep messing with the help." She smiled.

"Is that what she called you?" She could see the flash of anger in his eyes and a crease form between his eyebrows.

"No." She realized he would have defended her and felt bad for joking with him. "She just told me to stay clear of you. Dante, I don't want you to think that... Well, it's just that I've just come out of a bad relationship. I'm not looking..."

He laughed. "Neither am I, believe me. I think you realize I have too many issues right now to step into something serious."

She smiled at him, "Good, now that we have that all settled. I think it's almost time for dinner."

That little witch just couldn't keep her hands off him.

She'd given her plenty of warning. Dante was destined for greater things than a mousy nurse who didn't know how to do anything. Maybe it was time to step up her game?

Her plan hadn't worked out so well with Katie, and looking back at it, she'd been a fool to hire the two dumb thugs. It was a good thing they hadn't known who she was, or they might have exposed her. Even if they had, she would have handled it. After all, what was the point in having the family position and prestige if you couldn't exploit it?

Yes, her plans with Katie Derby were over. The girl hadn't made a play for the family's wealth and her brother's will hadn't changed. She'd overheard Damiano saying to Kathleen that he had no intention of changing his will since Katie was taken care of by Roderick.

Dante's position was secure. Her mind flashed to an image of him as a young boy as she held him in her arms. Her precious boy. Her mind cleared. No, not in the flesh, but in so many more ways.

She'd been there from the first days of his life when his mother had disappeared back to the States and abandoned him. She'd been the one to feed him, change him, and keep him safe all these years.

Her years of planning would not be destroyed. She just had a few more plans to make. Maybe even this time she'd have to do some of the work herself to make sure everything was done perfectly.

Dante watched as Airlea closed and locked his French doors for the night. Her simple dark slacks, silver shirt, and the gold chain around her neck could have easily been a long, flowing dress made of silk and diamonds draped around her. He couldn't stop staring at her.

Now and then she would look over at him and smile. Did she know how she affected him? He hadn't lied to her earlier. He wasn't looking for a relationship. Hell, his longest relationship in the past had lasted only three months. He wasn't an 'in it for the long haul' kind of guy. Especially now when his body was broken, and his mind was not always sharp. He couldn't imagine trying to maintain a relationship with a woman while his own life was up in the air.

Looking at her though, he didn't have any problem thinking about enjoying a few pleasures with her. After all, she was there, good-looking, and she'd pretty much told him that she didn't want a relationship. Physical pleasures could be just what they both needed. A release.

He watched her walk over to him and take the tray from his lap. He'd eaten everything on it, quickly. It seemed like his body was trying to recover from the two days of not eating anything.

"Do you think you could go without a pain pill tonight? I'm a little leery of giving you anything just yet." She stood over him.

He assessed the pain in his body. Starting at his left foot, he moved up his leg, up his hip, then to his arm and shoulder. He knew he wasn't in any shape to have a physical relationship with anyone at the moment, but that didn't stop him from wanting it or from trying. After all, he was a man, and a horny one at that, and there were other things they could do to relieve their tension, at least for the moment.

"The only pain I'm in right now, you can help me relieve." He smiled at her and watched as she licked her lips and looked at him. He was wearing his basketball shorts and nothing else. His shoulder still hurt too much to try and get a shirt on, plus it was still warm enough he didn't mind being bare-chested.

He'd caught her looking at him several times and had silently made a note to ask her to bring up some of his weights from the garage. He may not be able to lift with his left arm yet, but he could at least work out his other side. He didn't want to let himself go while he was recuperating.

"Dante, I don't normally just jump into bed with someone—" She started.

"I never thought you would," he interrupted. "I hope you don't think that about me, either."

She smiled and moved to set the tray down on the desk next to the door. Then she turned and started walking around the room. "So, I was thinking about this. I know that you are in a great deal of pain, and I don't think that too much physical strain would be good right now."

"Airlea?" He groaned.

She stopped her pacing and looked at him.

"Lock that door and come over here." He patted the bed next to him and smiled.

He watched her eyes roam over him and felt himself getting harder. She turned and flipped the lock on the door, then walked over, removed her shoes, and slid next to him on the bed.

"Let's try and see how far we get before the pain is too much, shall we?" He pulled her closer and kissed her. He could lose himself in her lips. They were plump and soft.

He ran his hand down her braided hair and fumbled with the small tie that held it at the end. He wanted her hair in his hands and as he untwisted it, he couldn't help but marvel at its silky, softness.

Her hands were exploring his chest and he moaned when she started pinching his nipples lightly.

"You have such a nice chest." She moaned into his lips as she moved into a better position so that now she was leaning over him. One of her hands rested on the headboard and the other roamed his chest and neck freely.

He still had his good hand fisted in her hair as his bad arm lay by his side. He wished he had full motion in his shoulder, so he could pull her down to him. He moved his hand down her shoulder as he took the kiss deeper. She smelled like heaven. Now that her hair was freed, he could smell the zesty shampoo and wished he could bury his face in the soft curls.

"Airlea, you smell so good. I want to lick you all over." He watched as her eyes darkened and felt her soften over him. Running his hand down her side, he smoothly dipped his hand under her shirt and started to pull it up and off, which he discovered was very hard to do with just one arm.

She sat up and straddled him, making sure to sit higher on his lap, above the metal brace near his knee. Then she removed her shirt quickly, revealing herself to him. His mind fogged. He'd never seen more perfect breasts than the pair that were a few inches from his face. Leaning up, he started running his mouth over the soft skin and realized she tasted even better than she smelled. She leaned into him and wrapped her arms around him so that he was sitting up a little more. Their cores were pressed together, and her hips started to move slowly against his.

"Dante," she moaned and threw her head back as he took her nipple into his mouth. He sucked and then licked his way across to the other side. All the while her hips kept moving slowly over him, and he could feel that he was on the verge of coming. His hand reached around and grabbed her hip, to hold her still. How could she have him there so fast?

"Airlea, let's just…" he started. Then he moaned as he felt her slide her hands down his stomach, past the waist of his shorts to grip him. He swore his heart rate tripled as she started to move her hand over him.

Closing his eyes, he laid his head back on a moan and tried not to come too quickly. It had been over six months since he'd had any pleasure with anyone. He supposed it was the long hiatus that had him moving much quicker than he'd like.

"God, you feel so good." She ran kisses down his exposed neck, down his chest as she continued to torture him.

He moved and took her wrist in his and pulled it up and off him. Then he smiled at her and unbuttoned her pants, slipping them down off her hips. He watched as she took over and slid them the rest of the way down and off her long legs. Her skin glowed in the soft light of the room. He pushed her down until she lay beside him, then he rolled onto his bad side, only flinching a little.

"Dante?" She asked.

"No, don't. I'm okay." He smiled down at her. "Let me, I just want to please you."

She watched him with her dark eyes as he bent his

head and took her nipple into his mouth again, his right hand roaming her body and lightly playing over the lace panties she wore. He rubbed her softly through the light material until he felt the moisture through the lace.

Her hips moved up and down with each stroke of his hand. Her hands fisted in his hair as he kissed his way up her neck and back to her soft lips. Then he pushed the lace of her panties aside and touched her silky skin. Her shoulders jumped off the mattress as she moaned into his mouth. He rubbed her slick, soft skin until finally he dipped one finger into her heat and had her coming in his hands.

When he felt her stop convulsing, he moved his hand up to her chest and rolled her nipple between his fingers. Her eyes opened, and he watched her as she ran her hands down his chest and pushed him onto his back. Slowly, with her eyes on him, she pulled his shorts lower until his erection sprang free.

"Mmm." She smiled at him, then shocked him as she leaned down and took his entire length into her mouth smoothly, licking him as she moved up and down. He leaned his head back and kept eye contact with her as she pleasured him.

He'd had his share of women in the past, but none had ever been this good at what Airlea was now doing to him. She was using her hands and mouth and he didn't think he could hold out much longer.

"Let go, Dante, just let go," she said against his heated skin.

How could he deny her? Why would he want to? Just then lights exploded behind his eyes and his entire body tensed as she pleasured him to completion.

❄

Dante fell asleep immediately, and Airlea couldn't blame him. She knew that he had overextended his energy that day. They were lucky they hadn't hurt him. He was half laying on his damaged leg and shoulder and she was afraid that if she tried to roll him over, she might wake him, or worse, cause him pain.

She lay there for just a few minutes, watching him sleep. His dark eyelashes and mouth were mesmerizing, and she couldn't seem to look away. Her eyes traveled over his body and she marveled at how great of shape he was in. She knew some people with major injuries like this let their bodies go. She'd have to add some other exercises into his daily routine. Knowing how much he could handle allowed her to make sure she pushed his limits.

Slowly, she moved to get off the bed and gather her clothes. She'd enjoyed the release—no, she'd needed it. She wasn't one to ever deny her needs and knowing that they were on the same page as far as not wanting anything more personal allowed for a wonderful outlet. Making sure she turned the lights down, she peeked out the door to make sure no one was in the hallway. It was darker there as she made her way the few steps to her room without incident.

Smiling, she decided to treat herself, even more, that night and went into the bathroom to run hot water for a bath.

irlea was in a dead sleep when she heard the thud. She jolted from the bed and listened, then her mind registered moaning and she rushed from the room, down the hall, and flew through Dante's door.

Seeing his bed empty, she ran to the other side and saw him looking up at her through the darkness. Rushing to switch on the nearest lamp, she asked. "Are you okay? What happened?" Seeing him lying face down on the rug, still, bare naked, she bent down to help him up.

"Get your hands off him!" She hadn't heard his aunt move into the room, and she was shocked when her arm was yanked back, and she was pushed a few feet away. "I told you to leave him alone, now look what you've done. No doubt he's ripped another stitch out fooling around with you."

Dante's eyes were huge as the woman pulled him from the floor. His mouth opened and closed a few times and Airlea watched with some humor as he tried to shield himself with his good hand from his aunt's view.

"Aunt Florentina, we weren't doing…" He started.

"You be quiet now, I'll have my say. This woman is standing in your bedroom, in that outfit in the middle of the night and you are not going to lie to me and tell me you weren't doing anything. I won't stand here and have you lie to me. No doubt it's her fault you are on the floor." The older woman's face was red and her voice was so loud that the whole house could probably hear every word. Her long gray hair was tied back in a loose braid and her night coat was zipped up to her chin. Airlea questioned if the woman had ever been pretty or if she'd just quickly gone from a young woman to an old maid. That got her wondering if she'd ever been with a man and what kind of man would have her.

She watched as his aunt helped him sit back down on the side of the bed. He quickly covered himself with the sheet and blanket and was no doubt silently wishing for his bathrobe.

Airlea walked over and took it off the hook and handed it to him, then turned and addressed his aunt. "Miss Cardone, I was in my own room when I heard Dante fall. I got in the room seconds before you did. I assure you, up until a few minutes ago, I was resting peacefully in my own bed."

"You expect me to believe you? Dante?" His aunt looked down at him, waiting.

Airlea saw Dante question it. The last time he'd seen her she was lying naked next to him, happily pleased. He turned to his aunt.

"I simply fell while trying to go get a glass of water. For a minute I had forgotten my injuries. That's all. Besides, my private affairs are none of your concern." Of course, he made this statement right as his mother and father came rushing into the room. Airlea closed her eyes and took two deep breaths.

"What is going on here? Tina?" Damiano asked, using his nickname for his sister. Airlea wondered if anyone else had ever called her that, but by the look she gave her brother, she wondered how he even got away with calling her that.

"This *nurse* has seduced Dante and because of their rowdy behavior, he has ended up on the floor, hurt. By the looks of him, he's in a great deal of pain. No doubt she's forgotten to give him his pain medicine again." The woman walked into the bathroom and Airlea could hear her hunting around the drawers.

"Dante are you in pain?" Airlea asked.

"I wasn't, but that fall jolted my leg some. Do you think it's all right for me to have another pill yet?" He asked.

Airlea looked at her watch and calculated. He'd eaten enough that day and it had been over two days since his last dosage.

"We should be fine." She walked into the bathroom and wasn't surprised to see his aunt still hunting through the other drawers. Airlea slipped the gold chain over her neck and unlocked the drawer. She took out one pill, placed the bottle back in the drawer, and locked it. Once she put the chain back over her neck, she walked to the sink and filled up a glass with water, all under the close eye of Florentina. Airlea could feel the woman's stare burning into her back.

When she walked back into the room, Kathleen was sitting next to her son, checking his bandages. It was almost time to remove them completely and let his incisions breath.

"Here, Kathleen, let me do that." She walked over and handed Dante his pill and the glass of water. "It's about time we stopped putting bandages over his incision points anyway."

She sat and took over the task. "Well, nothing ripped this time. They actually look quite good. No doubt when we get the staples out tomorrow the doctor will be pleased."

"Well, as long as you're okay, son, we're going to head back to bed. Florentina, go back to bed." Damiano didn't even look back as he and Kathleen walked from the room. Florentina followed them quietly. At the door, she turned and kept her eyes on Dante.

"Be more careful. I wouldn't want someone to get hurt." Then she turned and left, making sure to leave the door wide open.

Airlea looked at Dante. "I really was in my room. I left shortly after…" she nodded her head in silence. "I took a bath and was fast asleep when I heard you hit the floor."

He reached out and touched her hair, which was still damp from her bath. "I know." He smiled.

"Then why did you look like you questioned me?" She swatted at his hands. "You got me in trouble with your aunt. Didn't I tell you she warned me to stay away from you?"

He smiled, "Yes, but I can't help but defy her. Plus, it was very nice seeing you blush."

"I did not blush!" She reached up and took the glass from him.

"Yes, you did. I think I'll have to see you like that

more often. Let's see…" he reached up and scratched his chin. "What else can I do to cause your cheeks to flame?" He reached out and grabbed her and had her lying over his lap then his mouth was on hers. The kiss was fast and potent, and she couldn't help but melt into it, into him. "There it is, your whole face glows when I kiss you."

She smiled at him. "I like being kissed." She pulled back and looked at him. His hair was messy, and she wanted to climb into bed with him, next to his warm body, but she looked towards the open door and sighed.

He noticed her look and said, "Later."

"Yes, later. We need to focus on getting you on your feet first." She got up from his bed and straightened her silk nightgown.

"Have I told you that green is my favorite color?" he said, looking at her.

She looked down and remembered that after her bath she'd put on her silk nightie. She hadn't even bothered to grab the matching robe before she'd run into his room. She watched as her nipples peaked through the light material. Looking back at him, she saw that he had noticed, and a large smile spread on his face.

"Airlea, go lock that door." He growled.

Her mouth went dry at his look. No man had ever made her feel so wanted just by looking at her before. She was standing a few feet away and felt that if he continued to look at her like that, she would burst into flames on that very spot. Blinking a few times, she started to back up towards the door.

"I – I think I'd better go back to my room before your aunt comes back." She turned and left the room.

When she made it back to her own room, she leaned against the door and tried to get her breathing under control.

She knew he was in pain still and his mobility was limited, but she couldn't stop thinking about what it would be like to be with him. Lying in her bed, she drifted off thinking about what it would be like.

"No! I'm not going to do it." If he could, he would have stomped his foot.

It was the next day and Airlea wanted him to go down the stairs. His father and two hired hands stood there ready to help.

"Dante, you can do it. You need to get those staples out and you need to go into town to do that."

"I'm not going to try to make it down those stairs. I'll send for a doctor to come here and take them out." He stared at her.

"You're being childish." She stood looking down at him as he sat on the bed. His clothes, which she'd helped him dress in earlier, were quickly getting wrinkled. It had taken almost twenty minutes to get his pants and shirt on him, and she knew it would take almost that same amount of time to get them back off at the doctor's office, so the staples could be removed. "I suppose you could use the cane or they could try carrying—"

"No!" He glared at her and, holding onto the night-stand, he stood and held out his hand for her to grab a hold of.

"Slow down, just go slow." She watched as Damiano

stepped forward and took Dante's arm, allowing his son to lean on him.

They made their way out the doors and down the stairs. She held her breath as he took the first step, but they found a pattern and made it to the bottom where Kathleen and Florentina were waiting with nervous looks.

Airlea watched from the balcony as they loaded Dante up in a sedan, and then they all got in and drove away.

Knowing she now had a few hours to kill, she went back to her room, put on her tennis shoes and grabbed a sweater. Today she was determined to walk all the way to the pond.

She went to the kitchen and talked to Rosa and one of the maids as she packed a small lunch in her backpack and grabbed two bottles of water. When she stepped out of the back door, she was pleased to see Lucy sitting there waiting for her.

"Well, girl, it looks like we have most of the day to ourselves."

She enjoyed her daily walks with the old dog and usually set off at a quick pace, but today there was no rush and she decided to take her time making her way to the large pond.

Harvest season was in full swing. She'd seen several workers in the olive grove over the last few days, and today was no different. They had their baskets and ladders and when she walked by, she waved and smiled. Lucy trotted beside her as they made their way towards the hill and the pond.

The sky was clear today and she watched as a flock of ducks flew overhead, circled around, and landed in the pond. She had walked for almost an hour before she finally reached the pebbled shore of the pond. Lucy waded in and started to drink from the clear water. The ducks were still floating out near the middle and Airlea found a spot in the shade under a tall tree to sit down. She leaned her back against the trunk and pulled out a book from her backpack.

A little while later, she shared her sandwich with Lucy and threw some bread out to the ducks, who had ventured a little closer to her. She was standing by the water's edge when a shiver went up her spine and the hair on the back of her neck tingled. She only felt that way when she knew someone was watching her. She looked around but didn't see anyone. She was heading back towards her backpack near the tree when she heard something to the side of her. Lucy must have heard it too because she started growling and the hair on the dog's back and neck rose slightly.

"Hello?" Airlea looked around. There were trees and thick bushes that lined the other sides of the pond and she realized she didn't know if there were any wild animals around. Did the Cardone's have cattle or horses?

Walking slowly towards the tree, she bent down and picked up her backpack, then started back up the hill towards the house. Lucy watched her and finally started following her.

Airlea kept looking over her shoulder as she walked. Lucy seemed to be doing the same thing, stopping several times and looking back towards the water. Had someone followed her down there? She supposed that while she'd been reading, someone could have snuck up on her. She'd been very engrossed in her book and hadn't given any thought to watching out for other people. By the time she reached the top of the hill, she was out of breath and had worked up a sweat. She'd been walking at a faster pace since she was feeling uneasy.

She stood at the top of the hill and looked back towards the pond. There was no movement below. She could still see the ducks floating in the blue water and realized it had probably all been in her head. She'd lived in the city too long if simple country noises were spooking her. After all, she knew that rodents and other small animals made noises, too. Shaking her mind clear, she started down the pathway towards the orchard.

By the time she'd made it back to the house and had cleaned up, she was feeling pretty stupid about being spooked. Luckily, the only one to witness her little scare wouldn't go around telling anyone about it. Lucy had disappeared when she got closer to the house.

Less than an hour later, she stood on the balcony and watched the sedan drive back up the long driveway and park next to her smaller vehicle. Walking down the stairs to help Dante, she could immediately tell that he was worn out. She could see it in his eyes, which were dull looking and a little red.

"How did everything go?" Airlea asked Kathleen as she got out of the car.

"Oh, fine. The doctor seems to think that he is healing fast, and the pins are doing a fine job holding the bones in place. Here," she held out a few papers, "he gave me these to give you. It's a list of acceptable therapy tasks." Damiano took a crutch from the trunk, then he walked over and helped Dante out of the car and gave it to him. "He also gave Dante crutches, but he can only use one because of his shoulder."

Dante stood up and leaned on the crutch and smiled

across the car at her. Just then Florentina stepped from the car and stood between them.

"Shall we get you upstairs and back in bed?" Airlea asked as she walked around the car and helped Dante towards the outside stairs. He struggled with them, but by holding on to the railing with his bad arm and the crutch with his good arm, he finally found a system to jump up the stairs on his good leg. By the time they reached his room, she could see his energy was completely gone.

When he sat down on the side of the bed, she heard him release a sigh of relief.

"How is your pain?" She asked.

"It's fine, I'm fine, just a little tired," he said as she bent down and removed his shoes. "I can undress myself."

She looked up at him, "Is that what you want?" She was pleased when his eyes sparked a little.

"No." Then he smiled slightly and leaned back to watch her remove his shoes. She lifted his bad leg and gently moved it to the bed. He sat back and pulled his other leg up.

"I'll leave you to rest." She moved to walk away.

"No, please sit and stay a while." He motioned for her to sit next to him in a chair. When she sat, he asked, "What did you fill your time with today?"

She sat back and told him about her walk with Lucy. By the time she was done with her story, he had fallen asleep. She walked quietly from the room, going out the French doors. She went down the wide stairs and took the path towards the kitchen door. Lucy was there, sitting by the door in her favorite spot. Airlea stopped and bent to pet the dog. Lucy enjoyed being scratched behind her right ear, but when Airlea reached her, the dog started growling at something behind her. Then she heard a loud crash which caused both her and the dog to jump. Something heavy and sharp hit her ankle and she yelped. Lucy whined and ran off towards the garage with her tail between her legs. Airlea looked and saw that a large clay pot had fallen from the top of one of the pillars on the balcony.

Just then the back-kitchen door flew open and Kathleen and Rosa, rushed out, followed slowly by Florentina.

"What was that?" Kathleen asked. Looking around she noticed the plant. She must have seen the shocked look on Airlea's face. "Oh, my goodness, that almost hit you." She rushed to her side and grabbed her arm. "Are you alright?"

Airlea felt a little shaken. The pot was huge and heavy with dirt and plants. It must have weighed at least fifty pounds. If she had not stopped to pet Lucy, it would have fallen on her head.

Kathleen grabbed her arm and started walking her into the kitchen. "I don't know how that could have fallen. I had the gardener place them up there myself. He assured me they were all steady." She walked Airlea to a chair where she sat down without saying a word. "My dear, you look like you're in shock. Quick Rosa, get Airlea a cool glass of water." The frail woman rushed off as Airlea's mind ran over what could have happened had she not stopped to pet the dog.

"I – I stopped to pet Lucy." It came out as a whisper.

"What?" Kathleen patted her hand.

"I stopped to pet Lucy. It would have hit me, but I stopped." She repeated.

"Oh, my! That's it. I'm having Kenny remove all those pots from those pillars. We can place them on the ground level. I don't know what possessed me to place them up there in the first place." Kathleen got up to leave.

"We've always had them on the balcony," Florentina said from behind her.

"Oh, look, you're bleeding!" Kathleen leaned down and took Airlea's ankle in her hand. "Rosa, get the medical kit."

Airlea looked and saw a large gash across her ankle. It didn't look too deep and her ankle only hurt a little.

"A piece of the pot hit it." She said.

"Well, it doesn't look too bad. How does your ankle feel?" Kathleen asked.

"It feels fine. Please, I don't want to be a bother. I can clean it up myself." She started to get up.

"All right." Rosa came back and handed the medical kit to her. "If you need anything…"

"No, thank you. I'll just go clean up." Taking the inside stairs, she made her way back to her room as the incident kept playing over and over in her mind.

CHAPTER 8

*D*ante was sweating for the first time in weeks and he was enjoying it. His father had moved some of his old weights from the garage into his room. Doing curls with his good arm was just one of the small pleasures he could now work on. The doctor had told him he could start lifting light weights with his bad arm, but nothing overhead.

He had spent the last hour doing sit-ups and crunches, working out his arms as much as he could, and even working on his bad leg, all with the help of Airlea. She had even given him some pointers on exercises he could do. Some of them were a little girlie, like leg lifts and some yoga moves. He felt kind of stupid doing them but had to admit moving his body felt good. The blood flow was clearing his head and he could feel his energy level spiking.

It didn't hurt that she was doing the moves with him. She'd moved the chair and tables aside in his room to clear enough space for them to work. She had a little pink mat she used and explained that she did yoga every day, which got him wondering if she had a little, sexy outfit she wore when she worked out.

After working out with her, he started lifting weights and she sat back and watched him. This made him want to push himself more so that by the time his sets were completed, he was happily worn out. His muscles would be killing him by tomorrow, but it was worth it. He could feel them burning now and smiled knowing she'd been watching him.

"I'm sure you are used to a more intense workout. You'll get there. Maybe this afternoon we can go for a short walk in the yard." She said.

His smile faltered. He didn't like traversing the stairs, and he was still a little shaky using the crutch to walk around with.

"You need to get used to walking with the crutch before you move to a cane." She got up from the chair.

"I'm not going to use that cane and I won't limp." He growled out.

He watched as her eyebrows shot up. "Then you will need to focus on building the muscles back up around your injury. It will take practice, patience, and a lot of work."

"I can do it." He felt relieved that she believed him.

She smiled at him. "I'm positive you can."

He looked into her eyes and saw that she did believe in him. He smiled back at her and realized she was the first person to believe in him wholeheartedly. Sure, his parents were proud of him, and his aunt had always told him he could do whatever he had desired, but none of them had ever looked at him like he was fully capable.

Even when he'd taken over the office in Portland, his

father had sent a team of people to help him through the process. He'd ended up just being the boss's son who wanted to look like he was doing something important. He had never truly had full power over the company, and he knew it was due to his father's lack of faith in him.

He couldn't really blame him. Looking back at it, he'd been just a figurehead in the company. He'd run meetings and handled important connections with high-paying clients, but the important business decisions had been left to be made by the team of people working directly under his father.

He thought about his role in his father's business and wondered if he still wanted to work for his father. Then he looked across the room at his gorgeous physical therapist and asked, "Why are you doing this job?"

That question seemed to set her back. "This particular one or physical therapy?"

"Both." He sat up a little more.

"Well, I took this job because I had recently lost mine and our mothers were friends. When they set this up, it fit my needs at the time. I became a physical therapist after one of my cousins was injured when he was eleven. When he broke his leg, I spent the whole summer helping him recover and fell in love with helping people heal."

"Do you enjoy it?" He asked.

"Working with you?" She smiled, and he nodded his head.

"When you aren't throwing things at me, yes." She smiled.

"Why?" He couldn't explain why he was asking so many questions. He just knew that he wanted to know more about her, about what she did.

"Aren't you full of questions today? What's this all about?" She sat back down.

"I've been thinking about going back to school. When I found out about my brother, I moved to Portland to be closer to him and my father made me the head of his business there. I didn't really enjoy the work, but it was my duty as his son. He even enlisted my mother to tell me how much they needed me there." He frowned.

"Was it something you enjoyed?" She looked at him, waiting.

"No." He looked off out the doors towards the sunny fields.

"What do you want to do?" She asked.

He thought about it for a while, then answered, "Well, when I was ten I wanted to be Speed Racer." She smiled at him and he could see the joy in her eyes. He enjoyed watching the sunlight hit her hair and wanted to touch it, to run it in his hands. "I was going to college to become a doctor when I left school early."

"You could always go back." She suggested.

He blinked a few times and his mind started whirling. He *could* go back to school. Being injured had only sparked his interest in medicine even more. Watching the doctors and nurses, he'd studied their every move when he'd been in the hospital and had wished to be part of their daily routine.

"Maybe I will." For the first time in years, he was actually looking forward to something.

This was too much! She stormed away from the open

doors and marched off towards the garage. Listening to Dante talk with that girl upset her even more.

Walking over to the back side of the garage, she was happy to see that Gino was already there.

"What happened? I told you to deal with her." She whispered.

"The dog was with her at the lake, and she moved right as I knocked the planter over."

"Well, this is getting to be too much. If you can't handle her, there is no reason I see for keeping you around."

"I can take care of her. You hired me to do the job and I always finish my jobs."

"You'd better. She is getting too close and I don't like the foolishness she is filling his head with. Take care of her and do it in the next few days."

"Why don't you just fire her?" He suggested.

"Because, you fool, if my brother says she stays, then she stays. He's the head of the household after all. At least until Dante is ready to take over."

Dante watched as Airlea walked across the grass towards him. The fall colors were at their peak and she looked like she belonged among the bright red and orange hues of the leaves in the trees around the yard.

He didn't know how she'd moved into his mind so quickly, but she'd taken up permanent residence there since he'd first seen her. Maybe it was the fact that she was the only person he interacted with that wasn't related to him. After all, it was her job to see to his every need, and lately, he'd had more needs that only she could fill.

He'd enjoyed their little session the other night and looked for every opportunity to repeat it. He was feeling stronger every day and knew that it would only be a few more weeks before he was recovered to the point that she would think about moving on. He didn't think that she had anything lined up after this job. She'd told him she'd lost her job in Greece but had yet to mention if she planned on returning there afterwards.

The exercises she had planned for them today were taking a toll on his energy level. His left leg was throbbing, and his head was splitting from all the pain, which only messed with his mood even more.

"Pick your leg up, Dante," she said from across the grass.

"I am picking my damn leg up!" He stood on his good leg and teetered.

"If you fall, it will be your own fault."

He grabbed for his crutch.

"No! You can do this. It a simple task." She encouraged.

"I'm done." He hopped towards his crutch. "If you want to really work on my balance—"

"I thought you wanted to walk without a limp," she interrupted. "I guess that was someone else who told me that." She started walking towards the house.

Damn, she knew which buttons to push.

"What has this got to do with not walking with a limp? I'm not even working on the walking part. Just teetering on my damn leg." He frowned.

"Balance is the key to life. If you can't balance yourself on your good leg, how are you going to learn how to walk again?" She turned and looked at him.

"I don't need to learn how to walk again. I know how to walk!" He said, feeling stupid.

"No, you used to know how to walk." She stopped in front of him. "You don't have the same body you did the last time you walked. You need to learn how to walk with your new body. Your new body has pins holding bones together. It has muscles and nerves that are damaged. Just wait until those nerve endings start healing; you'll have phantom pains all over your body even in places that weren't injured during the crash because everything is connected."

She held out her hand for him to give her the crutch.

"Learning how to balance on your good leg will teach you how to protect yourself when your bad leg fails you. Since it's too early to start putting much weight on your right leg, we have to start building up everything, so we can prepare your body for the task of retraining it."

Thinking about it, he decided it made sense. Handing her the crutch, he balanced himself on his leg and hoped no one was watching. He felt like a fool and probably looked like one too.

"Tomorrow we are going to take a short walk." She smiled up at him.

"How short?" He teetered and almost lost his balance. Even though the ground was right there, to him it felt as if he were standing on a high wire.

"Steady. Focus on centering your energy." She took a deep breath.

"Where did you learn all this?" He had never put any stock into all that new age crap.

She looked at him and smiled.

"You think I'm crazy, don't you?" She held up her hand to tell him not to talk. "I know that look. I've seen it in many of my patients before. You have the classic, *oh great, she's going to fix me with magic,* look." Then she laughed. "Now you're looking at me like I'm going to fly away on a broom. It's not magic. It's science, physical certainties that have been tried and tested over the years." Then she set his crutch down. "Watch."

She bent over smoothly and did a backbend that had his mouth watering.

"When you condition your body to do something, it becomes almost habit for it to follow your commands." She moved smoothly into a handstand. "This is something I haven't done in years." She moved back into a backbend in another simple move and had his mouth dropping open. Then she stood back up smoothly like she'd been doing that every day of her life. "Now, if we can condition your body to believe that you don't walk with a limp, you won't. It's as much psychological as it is physical. If you tell yourself to limit your movements because of the pain, ten years from now when the pain is gone, your move-ments will continue to reflect that."

"What else can you do?" he asked eagerly, and she laughed.

"I bet you didn't even realize that this entire time you've been standing there, completely balanced." She nodded towards him.

He looked down at himself and realized she was right. His leg held strong under him and he wasn't even teeter-ing. He felt as strong as a sailor on the deck of a ship in stormy weather. Looking up at her, he smiled. "You are amazing."

"Why? Because I got you to stand on one foot in your own yard?" She laughed.

Later that evening, after spending a few hours on his laptop answering emails, he looked up to see his mother bring in his dinner tray.

"Where is Airlea?" He asked.

"We don't know. She didn't show up to take your tray. I have your father out looking for her. Rosa said she saw her going on her walk shortly after your session, but no one has seen her since. I hope she didn't fall and hurt herself."

He sat up a little straighter. "Is there something I can do? Do you have the others out looking?"

"Don't worry, we'll find her. She couldn't have gone far." His mother set the tray down.

"Is Lucy here? I know sometimes she walks with her." Dante suggested.

"Yes, she's downstairs. Apparently, she got left in the laundry room." His mother frowned.

Dante wished he could join the search for Airlea. "How long has she been gone?" He looked over at the clock.

"Almost four hours. I'm sure she just lost track of time. Don't worry. I'll have her come up and let you know she's all right. Eat your dinner. I'll go see what's going on." His mother left the room.

Four hours later, Damiano and the crew came back

without any clues to Airlea's whereabouts. It was a quarter to midnight and still, they hadn't heard anything from her.

"It's too dark out there, son. We'll have to continue our search tomorrow." His father said.

"Dad! She could be hurt." His concern laced his words.

"I know, but having my men out there in the dark, someone else could get hurt. We'll see better in the light, maybe pick up her trail." His father shook his head.

Dante didn't sleep at all that night. He sat on the deck and looked off into the dark night. He was thankful that the weather hadn't taken a turn for the worse like the weatherman had said it was supposed to. Around three in the morning, however, their luck changed. The rain started falling in huge drops and the temperature dropped another ten degrees. Lucy lay down beside him under the overhang as he watched the storm building. Then her head came off the ground and she sat up, looked at him, then sprinted off into the darkness.

Did Lucy know something they didn't? Where was Airlea? Was she injured? Was she lost? His mind played over scenario after scenario, each one worse than the last. He felt helpless. His broken body was not only hurting him, he was sure that if he wasn't injured, he would have found her by now. He just knew that he could have found her. Now more than ever, he felt the betrayal of his body.

She felt like a fool. How could she have gotten locked in the small shed? She had walked by it, and upon hearing what sound like an injured kitten, she'd walked in the unlocked door and looked around. Shortly after commencing her search for the animal, she noticed that the door had swung shut behind her.

After she'd searched the entire five-by-five shed and found no animal, she tried the door, only to realize it was locked. She tried to remember if there had been some sort of latch on the outside that might have locked. All she could remember was pulling a flat handle as she had opened the door. She spent the next few minutes trying everything she could to open it. She walked over to the window and tried to look out. She used a large barrel and box to try to climb up to it, but it was almost ten feet off the ground, and after realizing there just wasn't enough stuff to stand on, she gave up trying to get out that way.

For such an old shed, it was sure solidly locked up. After the first hours, panic had set it. It was time for Dante's dinner and she was getting worried that they would be missing her. How would she explain that she'd locked herself in a shed? How stupid would it make her look? She'd tried again to work open the door, only to come up short. She'd seen someone open a door once in a movie by removing them, but she couldn't even try that, because the hinges were on the outside. She'd tried kicking the door, pushing it, and she even tried to ram it with her shoulder, which had only caused her shoulder to hurt.

Sitting down next to a box and a large barrel, she tried to think of other ways to get out. It was cool in the shed and she was thankful she'd worn the sweatshirt as she shivered. She was getting hungry, but skipping a meal was something she'd gotten used to with her job at the hospital.

Her eyes kept going back to the small window. How would she get up to it? And once there, how would she climb out? Was there a large drop?

She leaned back against the wall and thought. By this time, it was dark, and she couldn't even see the window anymore. She kept listening for someone, just in case they were out looking for her, but she didn't hear anything. She must have fallen asleep because suddenly she was being jolted awake by a loud boom of thunder. She quickly backed against the wall. When the lightning hit next, she noticed the shed door stood wide open.

Had someone come? Then in the dark, she heard a low voice speak in thick Italian, "Come here, girlie." She scooted farther back, behind a large box she'd been resting her head on.

Fear froze her breathing. When lightning hit again, she saw a tall figure standing in the doorway. The rain pelted down on him and she saw he had something in his hands that looked like a large hunting knife. She was going to die. She just knew there was no way out of this. He must have seen her because the next time lightning flashed he was only two feet away, looking directly at her.

She saw dark eyes and the shine of the knife before it went dark again. She screamed and kicked out, hitting him in the shin. He didn't even slow down as he grabbed her with his empty hand and pulled her up on her feet. His hand was in her hair, holding her close, and the knife was at her throat. His foul breath hit her face and caused her to recoil. She could smell his stale body odor and tried to kick out.

"There you are, girlie. We're going to have some fun, you and I. No one's out looking for you anymore so you can scream as loud as you want. I want to hear you scream." He said right next to her ear.

She did scream, and he slapped her across the face

and yanked her around so her back was to him as he fumbled around grabbing her chest in a vise-like grip, bruising her. She tried to kick out and push his hands away as he ripped her sweatshirt, and just when he started to yank her pants down, she heard a low growl. He turned around, but in the darkness, she couldn't register where the noise was coming from. In the next flash of light, she saw Lucy standing in the doorway, her fur drenched and her hackles up, her teeth bared as she slowly walked towards them.

"Damn dog! Get back!" he yelled and loosened his hold on her. Now was her only chance. She dropped down out of his reach just as Lucy jumped towards them. She heard a yelp but didn't stop as she rolled. Once she was free from his hold, she ran out the door. She didn't know if Lucy was okay, but she knew she had to get out, knew she needed to get as far away as possible.

Dante heard her before he saw her. She was running and screaming, and he watched as she ran across the stone pathway.

"Help! Someone help! He's got, Lucy!" She kept screaming.

"Airlea! I'm up here. Dad!" Dante stood up, holding onto the doorway as he watched his father step out onto the balcony from his room several doors down.

"What's going on?" His father asked.

"It's Airlea!" Dante watched as she ran up the stairs, her sweatshirt was ripped and soaking wet. Her wet hair flew in the stormy wind and she had blood running down her cheek. She didn't stop running until she was in his arms.

"He's got, Lucy! I think he killed her." She sobbed into his shoulder.

"Where?" Damiano asked he had pulled on his boots and coat.

"The shed, across the olive grove. I think he locked me in there. I thought the door had just locked behind me, but now…" She buried her face into Dante's shouter.

"Shhh." Dante held her closer and looked over at his dad.

"I'll get the men and go check it out." He nodded.

His mother and aunt were there now, and Kathleen said, "Be careful." Then she kissed Damiano before he disappeared down the stairs.

"Here, let's get you inside out of the cold and get you changed." Kathleen took Airlea and walked her towards her own room. Dante grabbed his crutch and followed them.

"Where do you think you're going?" his aunt said from behind him.

"I'm going to make sure she's all right." He said.

"Your mother can take care of the girl. You need your rest." His aunt took his good arm.

He turned on his aunt. "I'm not a child. I can decide when I need rest or not. Right now, I need to make sure Airlea is all right." He turned back around and followed his mother into her room.

He sat on the chair by the door as his mother grabbed several towels and started to clean Airlea's cut, murmuring to her the entire time. He noticed there was a small gash across her neck.

"Here now, I've started a hot bath for you. You'll be all right now." His mother said, in a soothing tone.

"Can you tell us what happened?" he asked from his corner.

"Dante!" His mother looked over at him.

"No, it's okay. I'm okay." He watched with amazement as she took a deep breath and composed herself.

"I had taken a walk. Normally Lucy walked with me, but I couldn't find her, so I started walking by myself. I had made it past the olive grove when I thought I heard a kitten in the shed. When I got closer, it sounded like it was injured, so I went in to see if I could help. I thought that the door had closed and locked behind me, but… Well, I couldn't get out. I tried everything, the door, the window. Then it started to thunder and when I looked, the door was open and there was a man there. He had a knife. He said something about no one was looking for me so I could scream."

Dante stood and walked over to her. "Are you okay? He didn't…?"

"No, Lucy got there." She closed her eyes and he could see that she was shaking.

"Mom?" He waited until she looked at him, and he saw the tears in her eyes. "Stay with her. I'm going to check on Dad." She nodded. "I'll see you in a while," he said to Airlea. "Take a hot bath; mom will stay with you." When she nodded, he noticed the tears were starting to run down her dirty cheeks and he wanted to rip someone apart.

He walked from the room out onto the back porch just as his father came running through the yard, holding Lucy.

"Is she --?" he called down to his father.

"No, she's been cut, but I think I can stitch it up." He

ran in through the kitchen door. Dante maneuvered the stairs carefully, getting wet in the process. He should have gone inside, but he was so worried about the damn dog who had just saved Airlea.

He made it into the kitchen just as Rosa leaned over Lucy. They had laid her on the kitchen table and Dante could see the fresh blood oozing from a large gash on her flank.

His father had grabbed a handful of towels from the pantry and was trying to dry the dog off.

"Let me, dad." Dante went over and sat next to the table. Moving the chair, he positioned himself, so he could hold the dog down and dry her off.

"I'll get the medical kit. We'll need to close the wound." His father said.

It took them half an hour to clean and close the gash. Lucy whined, but after they had finished, she was resting peacefully. His father made a bed for her next to the fireplace in the living room and was sitting in his chair, watching her.

"Did you catch him?" He asked.

"There was no one there. We saw a lot of blood. Lucy must have taken a chunk out of whoever it was, but he was long gone by the time we got there. How's she doing?" His father nodded towards the stairs.

"She was shaken. I'll check on her in a while. Mom is with her now. She says that she thinks he locked her in there and waited until everyone was done searching. Dad, that means he was working for us. Is there anyone missing?"

His father stood up and stormed out of the room.

Fifteen minutes later he walked back in, he looked madder than Dante had ever seen him.

"Gino is missing. His stuff is gone." His father sat back down in the chair. "How's she doing?" He nodded towards Lucy.

"She hasn't moved. Her breathing is fine, though." He looked towards the stairs, wanting to know how Airlea was dealing.

"That's good. I'll kill the man if I ever see him on my property again." His father growled out.

He knew his father didn't make threats lightly, but he had to agree with him.

"I'll go check on Airlea." Dante stood.

"Do you need some help getting up the stairs?" His father started to get up.

"No, I've been working on it and I've got it down. Thanks, Dad." He smiled down at his father.

"Night, son." His father's eyes wandered back over to Lucy.

Dante got to the top of the stairs quickly and was impressed at how easily he had made it.

He knocked on the Airlea's door and opened it after his mother called for him to enter.

"How is she doing?" He walked in and realized his mother sat in the room alone.

"She's doing fine. She's taking a bath still. Did they find out who it was?" His mother stood.

"Yes, Gino. He's gone. Lucy was hurt, but dad stitched her up." He looked towards the bathroom.

"Oh, no, the poor dear. From what Airlea says, we owe that dog for saving her life." His mother's voice cracked a little.

He nodded and looked down at his mother. The worry was real. He remembered Airlea saying something about their mothers knowing each other.

"How do you know Airlea's mother?" He watched his mother look up at him and smile a little.

"Maria and I go way back. She used to be engaged to your father," she laughed, "and she was the nurse when I delivered you." She smiled and patted his hands. "She was the only person who knew about my secret life until it was all exposed last year. We stayed in touch and she's been a constant companion to me through all these years."

He looked at her and knew they had avoided talking about everything. It has been over a year since her divorce from the man she had cheated on with his father.

"Mom? Why did you lie to dad? Why did you keep your secret for so long?" He asked.

She took a deep breath and looked at him. "Dante, life isn't as easy for some of us. You've had your father and aunt by your side your whole life. Ric and Katie had their father, Rodrick. I've enjoyed all of you. When it all started, Rodrick and I had just separated. I thought I was over the relationship, and I quickly fell in love with your father. I've never fallen out of love with him. I believe that there are people out there that are destined to be together no matter what. I know what I did, lying to everyone, was wrong, but I didn't have the courage to stand up for what I wanted. It was easier, or so I thought, to play the game I had wrapped myself in. I love your father so much; I can't imagine not being with him. I can only hope that my children will find the happiness that we have found. I know that Ric has found that with Roberta and now Katie has Jason." She smiled up at him.

"Oh no, don't think about it. I'm not ready to even think about settling down yet." He shook his head.

She smiled at him. "You might be surprised. All I can hope is that when you do finally decide what you want, that you will have the courage to stand up and grab it." She reached over and brushed his hair from his eyes.

"He needs a haircut," Airlea said from the doorway. She was wrapped up in a large green bathrobe, looking soft and sexy, and he wanted to hold her in his arms all night, making sure she felt safe. "How is Lucy?" She asked.

"Oh, sweetie, Lucy is fine. You just come over here and rest. Dante will sit with you for a while. Won't you?" His mother looked at him.

"Yes, I won't leave you alone," he said. Airlea nodded her head and walked over to sit on the edge of the bed.

"Well, I'm going to go check on your father and Lucy. Goodnight." Then his mother left quickly. As she shut the door, he could have sworn he saw her wink at him.

They ended up talking for a while, then Airlea laid down in the bed and he sat by her. She hesitated at first, but then snuggled into his chest and quickly fell asleep. He watched her sleep and thought about what she'd been through. He'd always felt safe here at his family home. To have someone bring something so evil here … he shivered. He struggled with feeling that he hadn't done enough to help her. If only he were healed. But if he had never been injured, she wouldn't be here and he would have never met her, and he definitely didn't want that.

CHAPTER 9

*A*irlea felt like she'd been run over by a bus. Her back hurt, and when she looked in the mirror she noticed bruises forming all down the left side of her face.

Dante had slept quietly next to her. He had assured her it was for her protection and she hadn't complained. She felt safer with him in the room. She had cried all she could cry in the bath and she had to admit, it felt wonderful sleeping next to Dante, with his arms wrapped around her for protection.

She'd had that close call with Angelo but had never believed he would hurt her like the man had intended last night. She shuddered and tried not to think about what had almost happened.

"From now on, no more walks by yourself," Dante said over the plate of eggs that were propped up on his knees.

"You know, I heard you made it all the way down to the kitchen last night all by yourself. I don't see why you need to eat up here in your room all by yourself anymore."

"I like eating up here. Besides, I'm not alone." He smiled.

"Yes, well, maybe I would like to eat downstairs with the others instead of just grabbing a sandwich here and there. Lucy is doing better today. She's even up and walking around."

He smiled, then tilted his head and looked at her. She could tell he was trying to figure her out.

"I'm not that much of a puzzle, you know." She sat next to him and started eating her plate of food.

"Yes, you are. You're a gorgeous woman who has picked a humble job and has a mysterious past." He looked at her.

"Mysterious?" She laughed. "There is no mystery about my past."

"There is to me. You've yet to open up about yourself other than tell me why you do what you do." He said.

"What about you?" She turned to look at him. "All I know about you is what happened with your accident, and that you've lived in the States for a few years." She looked over at him.

"Okay, I'll ask a question, then you can ask one." He suggested.

"Oh no, I don't like this game." She went back to her food as he smiled. "I know how this one goes. You ask a simple, normal question, then I ask one, then your next question is one that is so embarrassing, I don't want to answer."

He laughed, "Okay, I'll keep my questions to non-embarrassing ones, then."

She looked at him and could tell he was being honest. "Okay, shoot. What's your first question?"

"Tell me about the last man you dated." He said.

She groaned inwardly. "Angelo was my biggest mistake."

"And?"

"And he is the reason I lost my dream job." She blurted out.

"Okay, now I need to know more details." He leaned back, crossed his arms over his chest and watched her intently.

"Angelo was one of the head doctors at the hospital I worked at in Greece. He'd been asking me to go out with him for over a year. Finally, after getting everyone's opinions about him, I decided to take a chance and go out with him. Shortly after, we started dating. Six months later, he moved in with me. Two days later, I kicked him out and broke up with him." She talked very quickly, trying to get the story out fast.

"What merited that?" He crossed his arms over his chest.

"He became very controlling and overbearing. In short, he turned into an ass." She smiled at him.

His eyebrows raised, and she could have sworn she saw humor there.

"Before you suggest it, no, it wasn't all in my head. He actually started going through my clothes and throwing away anything he didn't like. Then he suggested, none too nicely, that he be in charge of my finances, so he could control how much we saved."

Dante shook his head in dismay. "What happened with your job?"

"He'd been calling me and pestering me at work to give him a second chance. About a month after I broke it off, he showed up at my door and pinned me against the door. I dropped my backpack and kneed him. I made it into my apartment, okay, but I had left my bag out in the hallway. I watched through the peep-hole as he bent and picked up my bag, then walked away. The next day, my boss called me into his office. They had searched my locker and found my bag full of pills that had gone missing over the last few months. Naturally, they fired me on the spot without allowing me to explain. I was lucky they didn't call the police."

"I'm sorry that happened to you. It sounds like you're better off without him. How long did you work there?" He asked.

"Oh no," she shook her head. "You had two questions. Now it's my turn." She waited until he smiled. She knew he was thinking that her question would fall in the same line as his had, but she wanted to throw him for a loop.

"Tell me about the first girl you dated." She watched as his eyebrows shot up in question. "To me, the first person you date is more important than the last."

"Why?" He asked.

"When you're younger, your mind has built up the role that a significant other should fill. Taking the first step of asking someone to go out, you probably did a lot of thinking about her. She was the closest thing in your... How old were you?"

"Eleven years old." He smiled.

"Your eleven-year-old mind. I'd wager you did more thinking about that girl than the last four women you've dated."

He thought about it and nodded his head in agreement.

"Fair enough. Elizabeth was thirteen, and like I said, I

was eleven. She was the schoolyard bully. She had bright red hair and freckles all over her nose and cheeks, and when she cornered me one day after lunch, I blurted out that I loved her. I thought it was a better option than getting punched in the nose." He sat back and laughed. "I wish I had taken the fist to the face instead. But she grew up to be quite the beauty. I hear she went on to be a successful model of women's lingerie."

"You're making that up!" She laughed and leaned towards him, looking deep into his eyes.

"I wish. She made my sixth grade school year hell." They smiled at each other.

"Are you ready for a walk? I think we can make it all the way to the garage today." She smiled as he groaned loudly.

Florentina sat back and watched as Dante, holding onto the crutch, walked across the grass towards the girl like a dog would and felt her teeth vibrating with anger.

That fool. How could he have let her escape? She'd done her part by locking Lucy in the laundry room. Now, after the whole ordeal, she could tell that Dante was falling for the girl even more. And poor Lucy had been injured in the process. She watched as Lucy lay down next to Airlea and felt even angrier when she bent to pet the dog.

She could kill the man for hurting the dog and planned on doing just that. If he contacted her for his payment, she planned to take care of him herself.

After all, it wasn't the first time she'd killed, and it

wouldn't be the last. Her brother wouldn't be where he was today if she hadn't lit the fire and secured his future.

"Tina? What are you doing out here?" She turned and watched Damiano step out on the deck. Yes, she thought without remorse, to get what she'd worked so hard for, over the last twenty-seven years, she'd have to kill at least one more time.

That evening as Dante showered, he thought about his progress. It was slow going, and he was starting to get frustrated that he wouldn't be able to put his full weight on his right leg for another two months.

He was beginning to feel trapped. Trapped in his room, trapped in the house, trapped by his parents and his aunt. He knew they wanted the best for him, but the fact was, he wasn't getting any work done. Airlea was really the only person he enjoyed being around. His family came and went, but he was bored by their visits. They usually just sat and looked at him like he was broken, then asked him how he was feeling.

She was the only one who actually talked to him. He thought about how she had looked in the sunlight that day. She was a beautiful woman, but when the sun hit her, she glowed, her hair turned to amber silk and her eyes … her eyes looked like mocha and he wanted to jump in and never leave.

Then he remembered how she had done that back-bend in the yard the other day. She had obviously taken gymnastics as a child. He wondered how limber she was. He had to find a way to be alone with her. He knew his aunt was not pleased with his relationship. She'd always taken an interest in whom he was dating, more so than his own parents had.

He remembered once when he'd been dating a girl in high school. Emily was a sweet girl he'd worked up the courage to ask out, and they'd gone out on several dates and had even gone to a dance together. But after one date when they'd almost gone all the way in the front seat of his truck, she'd called him and broken it off. He'd assumed it had been due to her parents putting pressure on her to focus on her school work, but less than two months later she had started dating his friend Brad.

His aunt hadn't liked Emily. She constantly complained about how she was beneath him. Actually, if he thought about it, there hadn't been one girlfriend he'd ever had that had been good enough in his aunt's eyes.

"Are you almost done?" he heard Airlea call out through the door. He chuckled as he realized he'd been spending too much time in the shower. The hot water was helping relax his sore muscles. How could walking across the yard make his whole body hurt? Reaching up, he turned off the water and grabbed his robe.

When she helped him back into the room, he noticed that she had lit some candles. The room was dim and smelled of flowers on a spring day.

"What's all this?" he asked, sitting down in the large, soft chair by the doorway.

"I thought the room needed a little freshening up. Besides, how else am I going to seduce you?" She smiled down at him. He noticed then that she wasn't wearing her normal dark scrubs. Instead, she wore a light-colored skirt and a cream-colored top. One of her creamy shoulders was exposed as the shirt hung off it in a seductive arch.

"Honey, you don't even have to try. All I need to do is look at you to want you. Come here." He took her hand and pulled her down until she sat across his good knee, then he reached up and put his hand into her hair and slowly pulled her down until their lips met softly.

He'd thought about kissing her ever since the last time. Remembering how soft her lips were doing little to quench his appetite. She smelled better than the candles that were burning around the room. Her hair was soft in his hands, and he couldn't help himself from rubbing his fingers across the soft skin under her ear.

She moaned into the kiss and leaned closer to him. He felt her perfect breasts push up against his naked chest, then her hands were on him and he released his own moan. He felt her shiver when he traced the line of her neck with his mouth.

Her hands were pulling the robe off his shoulders. The tie was still tied around his waist, but she had successfully opened the top half to view him. His mind and mouth were busy, running his tongue up and down the column of her neck. She tasted so good, sweet, like honey. He pushed her shirt down and exposed her other shoulder as he continued moving his hands and mouth over her. She leaned back and ran her hands into his hair, holding him to her.

When he pulled her shirt down far enough to expose her, he was very excited to find that it was just her underneath the silky top. Her nipples were already hard, and he couldn't stop himself from dipping his head and tasting her there.

"I want you so bad," she whispered into his ear.

"God! Me, too." He moaned.

"Dante, I don't want to hurt you." She moved back.

"This damn leg." He pulled back and thought of the logic of having hot sex with a metal bar just above his knee. Not to mention that his shoulder was still supposed to be in a sling, though he hadn't put it back on after the shower. He had most of the movement back in it, and only wore the sling when he was walking so he didn't forget and move it wrong.

"Do you trust me?" She put her hands on his face and looked into his eyes.

He smiled and nodded his head.

"Good, come over to the bed and lay down."

"You're the boss." He stood up and she helped him hop the few feet to the side of his bed. Before he could sit down, she walked over to him, and with her eyes on his, took the tie to his robe and undid it. Then she ran her hands over his stomach, up his chest, and over his shoulders, pulling the robe off as her hands ran down his arms.

He watched her lick her lips and saw her eyes zero in on his arms and chest. When the robe dropped away, her eyes went to his crotch and she licked her lips again.

"Mmm, I'm going to enjoy this. Sit on the edge of the bed. Be careful with your leg."

He chuckled. "You don't have to tell me twice."

His hands went to her waist as she stepped closer. Her skirt was soft, and he ran his hands over her hips and rear as she leaned closer and kissed him again. He roamed lower, running his hands over her soft legs and lost himself in the silky, smoothness of her skin.

"Touch me, Dante," she moaned as her hands ran over his arms and stomach.

He pulled her skirt up until he found out that she was bare there, as well. He moaned into her mouth and took the kiss faster and deeper. Then she wrapped her fingers around his length as he found her with his fingers, and they both moaned.

She was hot and slick and he wanted to be inside her quickly. She moaned and leaned her head back, exposing her chest to him. He reached up and pulled her shirt aside, then took her into his mouth again.

He slipped one finger into her and she fisted her hands into his hair. Holding him to her perfect breasts.

"God! I need you, Airlea. Please." He said against her skin.

She pulled back and reached into his nightstand, removing a condom. "Let me," she said when he reached to take it from her.

She opened it and slid it on him slowly, expertly. Then she turned around, and facing away from him, reached back and held him as she slid down on his full length.

He couldn't think. Couldn't move. She was tight and felt so good as she slid up and down. He reached around and took hold of her breasts as he kissed the side of her neck. She supported herself on his good knee with one hand and the other covered his hand on her chest.

She moved slowly at first, her hips swaying, and then as her pleasure built, she picked up the pace. He reached around and found her slick heat and played with the tight nub there. She threw her head back and came just before he lost his own control.

He must have fallen back on the bed because a few minutes later, he felt her lift his bad leg up onto the bed. He opened his eyes and smiled at her.

"I'm normally not this tired after sex." He said.

"You don't have to explain anything. I can only imagine how tired you must be now. You'll build up your strength again." She smiled.

"God, I hope so!" He laughed.

He scooted up on the bed and patted the spot next to him. She shook her head at him and frowned a little.

"No, I need to go and stay in my own room." He watched her straighten her clothes and hair before she walked to the door. "Good night, Dante."

He watched her go and wondered why he wanted her to stay with him, in his bed, so badly.

CHAPTER 10

"Are you sure you're going to be okay?" his mother asked for the tenth time.

"Mom, I'm almost twenty-eight. I think I can handle a week on my own. Besides, Dad and Airlea are still here; it's not like you're leaving me all alone."

"No, I know that. I just worry about you. You've been through a lot in the last few weeks." When he gave his mother another look that told her she was being ridiculous, she continued, "Okay, fine. I know you'll be fine. Florentina and I will be back in a week." It was their annual trip to Venice and the spa, something they'd been doing together for as long as Dante could remember.

He watched as his mother left the room, looking excited. It was the one time of the year the women actually enjoyed spending time together. Usually, they tolerated each other's company. The weeks leading up to and after their short trip, however, both seemed to be happier than normal.

He supposed it had something to do with pampering themselves but tried not to think too hard on it. His father actually enjoyed having his sister gone for the short week. She was normally the one running the house, but since his mother's return, she'd stepped down and had been very quiet about the changes that had been made. Dante knew it was due to his father's influence.

It was weird, his aunt had always treated her older brother more like he was a king. Like he could do no wrong.

He remembered hearing his father talk about their parents once, Dante's grandparents. Dante never got to know them since they had died in a fire when he was three. But his father had said that they had been strict and had taught them to always follow the code of the old ways: a man was the head of the house and not to be questioned. He was just happy that his father hadn't enforced that rule with him.

Actually, the only one who had been strict with him growing up was his aunt. She had even demanded he go to the finest schools. Thinking about it, she was more of a mother figure than his own mother had ever been.

It had been a week since he and Airlea had found some time alone that night. She had worked him physically in other ways since then. She'd forced him to walk everywhere. He'd walked to the garage and had even walked the short path to the olive grove, which had been a huge challenge. He'd cursed her up and down that day. She had just laughed at him and told him to stop being a baby.

She had him start putting weight on his bad leg, though he could only put fifteen percent of his weight on it. She had him doing leg exercises that not only hurt but made him look like a girl. Looking down at his leg, he couldn't really complain. His leg muscle had turned very soft, very quickly after the accident. His left leg had looked skinnier and a different shade than his other leg, but now he could feel it was getting stronger and more defined again. In two days it would officially be one month since his accident, and Airlea said that she had a surprise for him. He didn't know what it was but waiting those two days was going to kill him. He was like a child wishing Christmas would come sooner.

Now he was thinking that they had a whole week together without his mother or aunt underfoot. He tried to think of something special to do for her. If he were in the city, and if it wasn't for his broken leg, he would have rushed out and bought her flowers or jewelry. He'd always been one to dote on the women he dated. He actually enjoyed picking out gifts for them. He especially liked picking out jewelry.

Each woman was like a puzzle, and he saw the hunt for the perfect item as a game. He thought about Airlea. She wore a gold chain around her neck with a charm on it. She also switched between gold and silver earrings. Because of her job, she'd didn't wear a lot of other jewelry. Then his mind cleared. He already had the perfect gift; he just had to walk down the hallway and open his father's safe to get it. The question was, how was he going to do that without alerting her?

Since the attack, Airlea had stopped taking walks, and she normally hung around his room most of the day. Once a week, she'd take her laundry downstairs to wash. But she normally did that on Wednesdays. Today was … He looked around and realized he didn't know what day it was. Flipping open his laptop he saw that it was Wednesday. His luck was holding out. He thought that if he timed it just right, he could make it to the end of the hall and get the item out of the safe before she came back up from the laundry room.

Swinging his legs over the side of the bed, he used his crutch and made his way down the long, tiled hallway. When he made it to his father's office, he was shocked to see his aunt sitting behind the desk.

"I thought you and Mom had left already." He said.

"No, we're leaving in just a few minutes. What are you doing out of bed?" She asked.

"I needed to get something out of Dad's safe. Besides, I'm supposed to be up and about now." He walked over and leaned heavily on the back of one of his father's leather chairs. He would never admit it, but he was tired from the short walk.

"What do you need out of your father's safe?" She asked.

He raised his eyebrows and looked at her. She was sitting behind his father's desk, using his father's computer like a pro. He hadn't even realized that she knew how to do anything work-related. She'd never shown interest in the family business before. But he supposed she might have taken part in the business at one point or another. Maybe after his grandparents had died?

"I'm getting Nonna's watch. The one on the chain." He said.

"What do you want with it?" His aunt's voice raised a little.

"It was given to me in her will." He suggested.

"I know that. I'm asking why you want to take it from the safe now?" She tilted her head and looked at him.

"Oh, I'm giving it to Airlea. I wanted to give her something to show my appreciation for all that she's done." He started walking towards the safe.

"You will do no such thing!" His aunt stood up and he watched her face turn an almost reddish-purple color. "We are paying the girl to do a job; your appreciation is in her check every week."

"Aunt Florentina, calm down. Nonna left me that watch to do what I want with it. And I want to give it to Airlea." He watched his aunt storm from the room without another word.

Walking over, he flipped back the bookcase and opened his father's safe behind the hidden wall. The watch sat in the same silk case and in the same spot it had all his life. Flipping open the lid, he looked at the small silver ball. Reaching in, he picked it up and flipped it open to see the face of the clock. It's simple, yet elegant design showed quality. He wound it and the hands started moving, keeping time, making him smile.

His Nonna had wanted him to have the watch for a reason. She'd left it to him in her will so that he would give it to someone he cared about deeply. Looking down at the small silver disk in his hands, he realized he cared for Airlea more deeply than he'd ever cared for anyone else in his life.

The watch was made for her. It was small and elegant. Its silver chain and small ball shape would easily fit around her neck, so she could keep it tucked under her scrubs. Plus, it was stylish enough to be worn out for the evening. Which gave him another idea. For this one, he'd have to enlist the help of someone else.

Just then, his father walked in with his aunt on his heels. "What's this all about you taking Nonna's watch out?" His father asked.

"Oh, Dad, there you are. Just the man I wanted to see." Dante ignored his father's question and the daggers his aunt was shooting at him with her eyes.

She had to step up her game. This was too much! Now he was giving that girl Nonna's watch. How dare he. She walked out to the car to wait for Kathleen to come out. They were supposed to leave minutes ago, but as always, Kathleen was dragging her heels.

She needed to do something drastic. She had to get the girl out of the house. Maybe while she was gone, she'd do some research into her and see if there was anything useful in her past.

Then she looked over next to the garage and got a wonderful idea. Yes, maybe she would enjoy her week away after all.

Airlea walked back up to her room with her laundry basket in her hands. Her freshly cleaned clothes were neatly folded and stacked in the large white basket. When she passed Dante's room, she peeked in to check on him and noticed that he was fast asleep.

When she walked into her room, she noticed her

silver dress was laid out on the bed with her black heels sitting next to them. She'd forgotten she had packed them. She'd only brought them along in case she had a chance to make it into Rome for dinner one night. There was a folded white paper laying on her dress. Walking over to it, she opened it and read the very masculine handwriting.

You are cordially invited to dinner in the main dining hall tonight at eight pm. – D

She smiled and fingered the smooth paper. So, he had decided he could make it downstairs for dinner, after all. Well, good. Picking up her silver dress, she held it close to her. She might just enjoy having him all to herself this week.

At five minutes until eight, she walked downstairs, feeling nervous. She didn't know why, but she did. Trying to shake off her nerves, she stopped at the bottom and took several deep breaths.

For god's sake, she'd eaten dinner with him for over a month up in his room and hadn't felt anything. Shaking her head clear, she continued down the hallway to the large dining room.

When she entered, she was shocked to see the room lit in candlelight. The large table had been moved and replaced by a smaller round one, which was covered with a white cotton tablecloth. A small bouquet of flowers sat in the middle with two sets of white and silver china place settings. Four taper candles were lit and sitting in the middle. Then she heard the music. It was soft and subtle and flowed through the room. There was a fire going in the large fireplace, which removed the chill from the room. Everything looked cozy and very inviting. The small couch had been moved to sit in front of the fireplace for a warm atmosphere after dinner.

Walking in, she looked around for Dante. Then she heard a noise behind her and turned. He was leaning against the wall looking very handsome in a dark suit. His hair had been cut and he was freshly shaved. The left leg of his pants had been cut to just above where his injury was. The rest of his leg was left exposed.

He had his crutch under his good arm and he was holding a bouquet of white roses.

"You look beautiful," he said as she reached up and took the flowers from him, knowing that he wouldn't be able to walk and carry them.

"Thank you. This is all so wonderful." She motioned to the room.

"I figured I *could* make it downstairs for dinner." He smiled and motioned for her to take a seat. He followed her slowly and when he tried to pull out her chair for her, she had to catch his crutch to keep it from hitting the floor.

"Sorry." He smiled as she took a seat, then watched as he took his seat and picked up a small bell.

Airlea laughed when Damiano walked into the room in a black suit, carrying two dishes.

"He's our waiter tonight." Dante smiled. Damiano set the two plates down and after bowing, exited while walking backward. Dante laughed at his father. "I think he's having too much fun playing his role."

"Would you like some champagne?" He took a bottle from the ice bucket sitting next to the table.

"Yes, please. You went all out, didn't you?" She said.

"It wasn't that hard. I did have some trouble moving the table." He frowned.

Her smile faltered, and she had a reprimand on the tip of her tongue. He shouldn't be moving anything.

"I'm kidding. My father had some men help him set it all up. I sat over in the corner like a good patient."

She smiled at him again. "Good, I'd hate to have to punish you."

She watched his eyes heat at the tease. Then she looked down at her plate and noticed a small silk box sitting next to it.

"Well? Are you going to open it?" He asked.

She looked up at him with a frown. Reaching up with one hand, she ran her finger over the soft case.

"What's this?"

"Open it." He leaned forward in his chair.

Reaching up, she flipped the lid back and saw an elegant silver ball on a delicate silver chain.

"It opens." He said.

She picked it up and opened the ball. One side flipped down to expose a feminine pearl watch face with black hands. She looked up at Dante, her heart beating too fast for her to count.

"Dante, I can't accept this. It looks old like it belonged to your family."

He smiled at her, "It was my Nonna's. I wanted to give you something to show you how much I appreciate all that you've done for me."

"It's my job, you're my job. I can't take this." She shook her head and set the watch back down in the box, closing the lid. She was so tempted to keep it, to try it on, but she couldn't. Just couldn't. She'd told him the truth. She wasn't ready for a relationship. She'd enjoyed sharing their pleasures together. But this…. She looked back down at the box. This was crossing that line they had both agreed they wouldn't cross.

Looking around the room again, she saw everything for what it was, what he was doing. He was trying to court her. To date her. She couldn't do that. She wasn't ready for it.

"Dante," she said, pushing the box towards him, "you need to save this for someone special. I appreciate the gesture, but I'm not that someone."

His eyes were dark, and she could see the anger and hurt. She'd expected it. What she hadn't expected was to see him smile again.

"Okay, it's okay. I understand. Shall we eat?" He nodded towards the food.

She was afraid that there would be an awkward silence for the rest of the meal, but instead, he surprised her with funny stories about his youth. He kept her entertained through the entire meal. By the time they walked over and sat in front of the fire, she was totally relaxed again and had almost forgotten the silk box that still sat on the table.

"So, what are our plans for the next few days? Do you have some more torture you've planned to put me through?" He smiled.

She laughed. "No, actually, I had planned on us taking Friday off."

"Really?"

"Yes, and don't ask why." She held up her glass and realized it was her fourth glass of champagne. Her nose tingled, a true sign she was on her way to becoming drunk.

"Why not? Are we going on another walk?" He leaned closer and played with her hair. She'd taken the time to curl it in tight little ringlets that scattered around her face.

When he played with them, running her hair through his hands, she felt like purring.

She leaned closer to him, "Don't ask." It was a whisper and when he leaned in to kiss her, her eyes slid closed to enjoy the feel of his lips on hers. He tasted as good as he smelled. She couldn't stop from running her hands over his smooth face, enjoying the angles.

"Dante, we should go upstairs." She whispered.

"No, don't worry, no one will bother us here." He said against her skin.

Her dress was short and when she felt his hands on her thigh, she moaned as he rubbed his hands over her sensitive skin. Running his hand up her leg on the outside, he cupped her butt. Then she moved to straddle him, making sure she was careful with his hurt leg, never removing her lips from his.

"Mmm, you taste so good," she said as she ran her hands over his shoulders, pulling his jacket off, then she got to work on the small buttons on his white shirt.

"My god, I can't seem to stop wanting you." He ran his hands up her thighs and when he found her, just her, underneath, he smiled. "Do you ever wear anything underneath?"

"Sometimes." She chuckled.

"I find that so damn sexy." He took her mouth again as he hiked up her skirt further and grabbed her butt, again.

She ran her hands over his chest and arms, enjoying the play of muscles and the light covering of dark hair. Moving her mouth down his neck she enjoyed feeling him shiver as she licked his throat. Then she reached down and pulled him free from his pants.

"Here, let me." He pulled out a condom from his back pocket.

She continued to kiss his neck and almost came right then when she slid down on him fully.

He threw his head back and groaned with pleasure. "My god, I could get used to this."

She leaned forward and took his mouth again. She didn't want to think about getting used to him, or to anything at this point. All she wanted was to focus on their pleasure, and hers was building fast. His hands were on her hips, pulling and holding her down.

"Airlea, come with me." He rained kisses over her face and neck causing everything to tingle. She almost saw sparks behind her eyelids as she threw her head back and exploded around him as he moaned her name.

When she relaxed down and rested her head on his shoulder, she closed her mind to the pure pleasure she'd just enjoyed. She'd been trying to fool herself that it had been like this before. But the truth was, she knew it had never been like this. Never.

She couldn't afford to get emotionally involved with him. She'd told herself that it was only for pleasure. Her mind whirled and she wanted to be alone with her thoughts. If she could just figure out what her next step was, she'd feel more levelheaded.

How could she have fallen for him so quickly? She'd only known him for a little over a month. Her mind flashed to Angelo's face and she stiffened, mentally and physically. She couldn't afford to chance trusting like that again. Sitting up slowly, she smiled down at him.

"Dante?" She watched his eyes flutter open. "I think we need to get you back up to your own room."

He smiled at her and she felt him grow inside her again.

"Mmm, in a minute." Then he leaned down and took her nipple into his mouth through the light silk she wore, and she lost all thoughts about moving. Except for rocking with his sweet motion.

CHAPTER 11

*D*ante didn't know why she was avoiding staying with him. She still slept in her own room every night, even when they spent hours after dinner pleasing each other. It was Friday morning and he was waiting in the kitchen for her to come down for breakfast.

Rosa looked at him funny, and he could have sworn she was happy for him. But when Airlea walked in, the smile disappeared.

"Miss Rossi, everything is ready for today," Rosa said and then walked out of the room.

"What's ready for today?" Dante asked Airlea as she sat down to eat her breakfast.

"That's for me to know and you to find out." She smiled, then stuck out her tongue at him and laughed.

"Oh, I see, keeping secrets?" He laughed.

"Only this one," she said with her eyes on her food.

"That's fine. I assume it has something to do with today?" He asked.

She sat and ate her food without looking up at him or answering.

"Oh, now I get the silent treatment." He reached over and took her slice of bacon.

"Hey!" She reached for it.

"Oh no. You don't get your pig meat back until I get at least one answer."

"Fine." She crossed her arms. "Yes." Then she held out her hand for her bacon.

"Yes, what?" He asked.

"Yes, it has to do with what we are doing today."

He leaned closer. "Fine, but you have to pay a toll." He pointed to his mouth and smiled when she leaned in and placed a quick kiss on his lips, then grabbed her bacon from his fingers.

"So when does this surprise take place?" He asked.

"After breakfast. You'll need to change." She looked down at the gym shorts and t-shirt that he usually wore. They were easy to get on over his leg.

"Dressed how?"

"The gray pants we cut up for you and a button up shirt should be fine. I know it's colder today, but I won't have you outside for too long." They had taken several of his pants and had cut off the left leg so he could easily get into more clothes. It left his whole left leg exposed, but he didn't care. He wasn't one to easily chill. Plus, the weather had been mild this fall.

An hour later he was not only excited, he was down-right happy. He sat in her small sedan and watched her as she reversed out the driveway.

"I'm glad your father had my car brought up here finally. Did I tell you it wouldn't make it up the driveway because of the mud?" She said as she drove.

"There have been plenty of times where I've had to walk the drive. I mostly just drove the truck all year long. Now that the ground is a little harder because of the colder weather, you shouldn't have too many problems getting up and down the driveway."

"Well, it's the first time I've left since I arrived. I can't wait to get into town. I've been too busy to even realize that I hadn't left since arriving."

He smiled. "I've been cooped up almost as long as you, minus the short drive to have my staples removed. But that didn't really count since it wasn't really an outing. So, where are we going?" He asked as she maneuvered down the bumpy drive.

"Oh no. You can rest assured that you are in good hands, but I am not going to tell you. You will just have to wait until we get there." They had just made it past the old tree that sat halfway down the drive and was heading towards the small bridge that covered the deep creek when she squealed.

"What?" He looked around.

"My brakes aren't working!" She frantically pumped the pedal. Her small car was picking up speed since this part of the drive was sloped downhill toward the creek bed. Then he remembered that there was a slight turn right before the bridge; at this speed, they wouldn't make it.

"Try the handbrake." He reached for his cell phone and punched auto dial for his dad's number.

"It's not working either." She was panicking and holding onto the steering wheel tightly.

"Dad, we're at the creek, the brakes are out!" he yelled into the phone, then threw it down on the seat.

"Dante! What do I do?" She was holding on tightly.

"Turn now!" He grabbed the wheel and they aimed the small car for the field to the right. He looked over at her just before they hit the ditch separating the road and the field.

Her head hurt, but other than that she was okay. She stood leaning on her car next to Dante, who was still seated in his seat. She watched Damiano fly down the drive in his truck. She waved at him, trying to assure him that everything was okay, that they were okay.

"What happened?" he asked, and she could see the love from father and son as Damiano jumped from the truck and rushed to his son's side. "Are you okay?" He knelt by his son's side, checking him over.

"Yeah, I think I just jolted my shoulder trying to help turn the wheel. Airlea hit her head." He looked up at her. She held a tissue to her forehead and when she realized the bleeding hadn't stopped yet, she put it back on the small cut. She figured she'd have a nice bump and bruise soon.

Damiano turned and looked at her. "Are you all right?"

"Yes, I don't know what happened. I had my car inspected right before I left Greece." She looked at her sedan. Its once shiny hood was folded up and destroyed as it sat front down in a small ditch. If it hadn't been for the rock and dirt in the ditch, they probably wouldn't have stopped so smoothly.

"Well, it looks like it's not too bad. I know a guy in

town who can fix it up. We can have it towed. Do you think either of you need to go to the hospital?"

Both of them shook their heads no. "It really was a somewhat soft landing. The dirt and rocks cushioned it. I think most of the damage is from hitting the ditch. Really, you would have gotten worse in a bumper car at the carnival." She was trying to reassure herself. The fact that her hands were still shaking didn't go unnoticed by either of the men.

Dante leaned up and grabbed his crutch from the back seat, then stood. "Come on, let's get back to the house. I'm sorry that our day is ruined. You'll probably want to call your insurance company."

She nodded and walked around to her side of the car and reached in the open door to grab her purse, then locked her door, making it to the truck just as Dante did.

On the ride back, she kept playing back everything that had happened to her since arriving there, over and over in her head. The potted plant, the attack in the shed, and now her car. Then her mind flashed to the day that Florentina had threatened her in the closet, and she felt a shiver run up her spine. She didn't think that the woman would stoop to the level of almost killing her. Besides, she had left two days ago with Kathleen.

Maybe Airlea had damaged her brakes on the trip here? The only time she'd had a rough drive was the day she'd arrived and had tried to make it up the driveway. Could something have happened when they towed her car up the driveway?

Then she started thinking about what could have happened had the brakes failed in town. By the time they made it back to the house, her forehead had stopped bleeding and she could feel a headache building. Her neck and shoulders were tense, and she wished for an aspirin and maybe a hot bath to relax.

"I'm sorry our day was ruined," she said, helping Dante out of the truck.

"Don't worry about it. Although I'm curious what the plan was for the day."

"We were meeting your sister Katie and Jason downtown." She sighed.

"Katie? You know my sister?" Dante asked.

"Yes. Surprisingly we met in Greece when I found Jason running in front of the hospital, carrying her. They had just escaped those kidnappers."

"Really?" He frowned.

She handed him his crutch out of the back of the truck. "Katie called here the other day and your mother told her I was working here. Katie and I had talked that night at the hospital, once Jason was checked in. I really liked her." She smiled a little remembering the conversations they had that night. "I'll just have to call her and explain what happened."

"I'm sure she'll understand. It would have been nice to visit with her when I wasn't all drugged." He said.

They walked into the kitchen and Rosa stood there, wringing her hands on her apron. The older woman looked worried and concerned.

"Oh, Cucciola mia! I'm so happy that you are both all right. Come, I'll make some tea and cakes." She motioned for them to sit.

"Please, first I should call your sister." Airlea pulled out her phone and dialed.

❋

Two hours later, Dante's sister walked in the front door, followed by her new husband Jason. He watched his father hug her and motion for her to enter. Then he turned and shook Jason's hand.

"I hear you've had an exciting day." Katie walked in, smiling at him. She hugged Airlea. "It's so wonderful to see you again. What a small world this is. I can't believe you're in charge of helping Dante recover."

Katie sat next to him, almost bouncing on the couch, and he couldn't help but smile at her. She was just so full of life. He didn't know what she was like before, but marriage suited her. He could tell she was happy and that was very important to him. Her eyes were almost identical to his, as were her chin and ears. He couldn't get over having someone look so much like him. Sure, he looked a lot like his father, but looking into Katie's face was something different. Here was a sister he'd never known he had. He'd found out about his half-brother Ric almost five years ago. But until last year when his mother had come clean, he'd had no idea he had a sister.

"We saw your car on the drive up. I can't believe that just happened. I'm glad you are both okay." Jason said.

Then Katie turned and looked at Airlea and asked, "So, tell me about my brother. Is he a terrible patient?" Everyone laughed, and all the awkwardness left the room. They spent a while catching up. His father excused himself an hour later, saying he was needed in the olive grove to finish up the harvest.

Katie had jumped up and asked so many questions

about it that Damiano decided to take her along with him. Jason stayed behind.

"I think it's good that they spend some time together." Jason was a pretty likable guy. His sandy dark hair was almost as long as Dante's had been a few days ago. His crystal blue eyes took in everything, almost as if he were still on guard, protecting Katie.

"I don't know what you must have gone through, protecting my sister. But I wanted to thank you. Without you, I would never have gotten to meet her."

Jason smiled. "Well, actually, your sister can pretty much hold her own. I think we made it through all that together."

"Whatever happened to the men who tried to kidnap her?" Airlea asked.

"They're going to trial later next month. Apparently, they didn't know who had hired them, since they never met the person face to face. All they could tell the police was that it was an Italian speaking person. They didn't even know if it was male or female."

"You haven't had any problems since then?" She asked.

Jason shook his head. "No, but that doesn't mean we aren't on guard. Actually, we hired Ethan, Ric's brother-in-law to try and track down who had hired them. Apparently, Ethan is ex-military and has been doing this kind of stuff his whole life." Jason laughed, "When I first met the man, I thought he was going to snap me in half."

Dante sat forward, "What do you mean?"

"The man had arms like an elephant's trunk, hands like boulders. After meeting him and talking to him, I don't doubt that he's the best. You know that senator's son that went missing a few years back?"

Dante remembered the news story. It was a national story. The kid had been playing on the school playground one minute and was gone the next.

"Ended up being a teacher, right? Trying to get a few million in ransom."

"Yeah, that's it. Ethan is the one that tracked the guy down. Saved the kid just in time, too." Jason smiled.

Dante let out a whistle. "This is Ric's wife's brother?" Dante thought about it. He supposed he was his brother-in-law in a roundabout way.

"Yeah. Anyway, he's been looking into the phone logs between the two men and whoever hired them. He's close to finding out where the calls were made from. He's even tracked down the two calls made to Rodrick and Ric demanding the ransom." Jason shook his head. "I tell you, the man is good."

An hour later, Katie walked in on the arm of her father. Their smiles were almost identical, and Dante could tell that the hour together had done wonders for the pair.

Since his mother was gone for the week, Katie and Jason decided to stay the night in one of the guest rooms. He knew that his sister still had issues with their mother. He couldn't really blame her. When he thought about it, he still had issues with her, too. But he'd never been given the chance to really become close to her like Katie had. She'd been a part-time mom to him and a full-time mom to Ric and Katie. If it wasn't for his broken body, he'd probably be in Portland now, working and living on his own, not having to deal with his mother that often.

Did he really want to go back to that life? When he

thought of his future, he could only see a few things. He knew he had to finish recovering, but he couldn't imagine his life back in Portland again. His apartment there didn't feel like home, hadn't ever really felt like home. Looking around the room, he realized this was no longer home, either. He still thought of Italy as his home, though, and didn't know if he would ever return to the States. He'd enjoyed living there for a few years, but there was just something about coming home and feeling like you belonged. Plus, he couldn't stop thinking about Airlea.

When he'd had his first accident, trying to stop the kidnappers from taking Katie, he'd thought only of his sister. Today, when the car had hit the ditch, his only thought had been of her. He hadn't cared what happened to him, he'd just wanted to make sure she was okay.

He didn't know what he wanted to do a year from now, ten years from now, but he knew he wanted to spend as much time with Airlea as he could. He wasn't ready to settle down, not like his sister and half-brother had. At least he didn't think he was ready. He had been giving serious thought to going back and finishing school. After all, he was only a few semesters away from graduating with a medical degree. Why not?

He had done some research and he could start taking some of those classes online until he healed enough to get back to school. The more he thought about it, the more he wanted to do it.

An hour later, they all sat around the large dinner table, laughing more than Dante could ever remember laughing in his entire life.

Not only was his sister smart and witty, she was just downright funny. She had this quirky way about her.

Airlea had asked how she and Jason had met and she'd recounted the story. He'd never enjoyed a story more and listened how Jason had saved her from drowning. Of course, her story and his didn't match but watching them, he could tell that the small argument they had about it over their dessert was something they did all the time. The entire time, they were holding hands under the table and smiling at each other. He was very glad that his sister was happy.

"So, where are you guys going now?" Airlea asked.

"Well, we're planning on heading back to the States soon. Jason's mom is still in Boston. We may settle down there, or head up to Portland to be closer to Ric and Roberta. Roberta is pregnant, and the baby is due next summer. I can't wait to be an aunt." Katie sighed. "I am so going to spoil that kid." Katie smiled, then looked at Dante. He was just taking a drink of his water when she asked. "You don't have any kids, do you? I mean, I could already be an aunt."

He choked on his water. He tried, really tried, to recover quickly, but Airlea ended up having to pat his back a few times before he got his choking under control.

"No," he coughed out and shook his head. Then he swallowed and tried again. "No, I don't have any children."

"Oh, well, then, I suppose this will be the first." He watched as his sister looked at Jason and smiled. Then he wondered if they were planning on having kids soon and, of course, he started wondering about himself. He'd never really thought about having kids. Oh, he supposed some-where in his future he'd always imagined having some. A boy to play ball with, a little girl with dark eyes and hair that glowed in the sunlight. He shook his head clear of the image he'd painted in his mind of his and Airlea's children. Reaching under the table, he found her hand and wrapped his fingers around hers. She smiled at him and he knew he'd found what he wanted for his future.

CHAPTER 12

*D*ante tried to be as quiet as possible, but walking down the long, dark hallway with a crutch and a bowl of chocolate pudding was very hard. He'd just made it to his door when it flew open.

"Where have you been?" She stood in his room, her hands on her hips, looking very sexy. He forgot about breathing. "I came to check on you and was worried sick."

He just looked at her. The light was shining behind her and he could see through her pale pink, silk nightie. Her hair was down around her shoulders, and she'd nibbled on her lips, so they looked fuller and very pink. He almost dropped the bowl of pudding. Luckily, she walked forward and grabbed it from him, then turned and walked back into the room. He followed her, shutting the door behind him and flipped the lock.

"You came in here to check up on me, wearing that?" He walked towards her. At that moment, he wished his leg wasn't broken and that he could make it across the room with her in his arms. He watched as she backed up and was pleased when excitement crossed her eyes.

"What…?" She started to ask.

He noticed that she was still holding the bowl of pudding. Reaching into his robe, he pulled out the can of whipped cream.

"If you want to share my dessert, we'll need some whipped cream, don't you think?"

She held the bowl up. "Dante?" She kept backing up until her knees hit the side of his bed.

"Hold real still, I wouldn't want to get any of this on you." He smiled, knowing exactly what he wanted to do with the can of cool whipped cream. He shook the can and stood before her, dropping his crutch on the floor. She stood still, holding the bowl between them.

Lifting the can, he put a little of the cream on her bare shoulder.

"Oops." He dipped his head and licked it slowly off her soft skin.

Her head fell back, and she moaned, "Dante."

"Yes?" He dipped his finger into the chocolate and held it out for her. Her eyes met his, then she leaned forward and licked the dark richness from his finger. He closed his eyes and moaned at what she was doing with his digit. She wrapped her tongue around it, then ran her teeth gently over it, finishing it all up by licking it clean.

He took the bowl from her and set it on the nightstand, then pushed her slowly down until she sat on the edge of the bed. He leaned over her and pulled the thin strap down her shoulder until she was exposed to his view. In the soft light, her skin looked like it glowed. She moaned and closed her eyes, rolling her head back as she leaned on her hands, which pushed her breasts up and towards him. He shook the can and placed a dab of the cream on each nipple, then set the can down and carefully got on the bed next to her. She looked at him through her eyelashes and smiled.

"I love dessert," he said, just before he dipped his head to enjoy her. He took his time running his mouth over her. Using his hands, he pulled the soft material aside and, in his haste, to expose her, ripped her nightgown.

He watched her eyes heat and saw her bite her lip.

"My turn." She pushed his good shoulder until he leaned back. She took the can of whipped cream and shook it as she used her other hand to push his robe from his shoulders.

He was naked underneath and he watched as her eyes sparkled with excitement and desire.

She sprayed whipped cream over his chest and bent to lick it slowly from him. He leaned back against the bed, giving her access. Her tongue ran down and across his chest, and he wanted nothing more than to take her quickly. He rolled over and bumped his leg, flinching just a little, but continued until he was positioned between her legs. Right where he wanted to be.

He smiled when her legs came up and wrapped around his hips. Then he ran kisses along her collarbone, across her slender shoulders, and up her soft neck. She smelled like spices and flowers and tasted even better. Closing his eyes, he felt her soft skin next to his and marveled at the differences. She rolled her hips up and he entered her quickly as she moaned with delight. Her hips moved, rotating, as he pumped in and out of her slick heat.

She reached up and gripped his hair to pull his head

down to her mouth. He held her close while he pumped into her.

"God, Airlea, I can't hold back."

"Don't. Come with me, Dante." She held him close and when he couldn't stand it any longer, he put his face in her soft hair and let himself go.

He was a lot heavier than he looked, but she enjoyed running her hands over his backside. They were slick with sweat and a little sticky from the whipped cream.

What had possessed her to play with him? She'd never done anything like that before, using food to pleasure someone. Smiling at the ceiling as she watched the shadows and listened to the cold wind outside, she wanted to do it again. He seemed to bring out the inner horny in her. She could feel his breath on her neck, which gave her goosebumps down her arm, and wondered if he was asleep.

"Stay with me," he mumbled sleepily into her hair. A million things flashed through her mind. Questions, so many questions she didn't want to think about it. She didn't want to take the chance. He must have felt her tense, and he rolled over onto his back to look at her. She noticed that his hair kept falling into his eyes. Pushing it back with her hands, she smiled at him.

"I can't." She said.

"Why not?"

"Dante, you and I know that we just wanted some fun. I can't stay, because I don't want to. I can't take that chance." She said, holding herself still.

He rolled over and she watched as he flinched a little.

"Did you hurt yourself?" She sat up a little.

"Forget my damned leg," he spat out. She could tell he was hurt and realized he had probably crossed the line they had set. She felt bad, she really did, but she just couldn't go there.

Bending down, she found her nightgown and saw that only the one shoulder strap was ripped. Pulling it back on, she got up from the bed. He lay there and watched her.

"I can't forget your leg. That's why I was hired. To take care of you. To make sure you heal and get back on your feet."

"Well, I'm on my feet." He sat up a little, holding himself up on his shoulders. She could see the anger and the hurt in his eyes. "Your job is done. So, why don't you just go?"

She smiled and sighed. Maybe it *was* time for her to go. She knew he still had a long road ahead of him, but really, at this point, he probably needed to go into a physical therapist who had access to the equipment he would need to help him get better.

"Goodnight. I'll talk to you in the morning."

She walked from the room quietly and when she got to her own bed, she cried silently into her pillow.

Ethan had spent the last few days looking at the computer screen. He was glad that he actually had some field work to do now. This hadn't been his normal type of job. Tracking down the people who had tried to kidnap his brother-in-law's half-sister was personal.

He watched as the man he'd been following entered the old building. If he was going to make a move, he'd have to do it now. Quietly, he moved from the spot he'd been sitting in for over two hours. The chilling rain beat down on his covered head. His clothes were soaked, and he was very cold, but he'd been moving his body, keeping the blood flowing for the last hour since the rain had started. When he stood, he quickly and silently moved to the window and watched as the man moved around the small room.

It took less than a second for him to barge in the back door. The man had no time to react before he was on him.

Speaking in Italian, he asked the questions that he needed answers to. Less than five minutes later, he exited the room with a new mission and a new life to save.

It had been just over a week since her car had been destroyed. Thankfully, her insurance company had quickly delivered a rental until hers could be fixed. She sat in the newer car and felt nervous. She knew she needed to secure her future and knew there was nothing left in Greece for her to go back to.

Looking at the large, stone building she was parked outside of she realized she hated interviews. She was still excited, but she was also nervous.

When she walked into the director's office for her interview, the first thing she noticed was how much nicer this facility was than where she used to work. The floors had new tile, the walls were freshly painted, and none of the lights flickered like at her old hospital.

"Miss Rossi, please come in. They are ready for you." The young secretary had said, motioning for her to enter the door.

She walked into a room full of men. They sat around a large table and all looked bored like they'd rather be anywhere other than here.

Half an hour later she walked out more nervous than before. Of course, one of the first questions they had asked her was what had happened at her old job. She'd done the best to explain it and thought that they had actually listened, all except a few who had looked down their noses at her. She did like the director; he seemed friendly enough and she thought she'd won him over.

She answered question after question and felt very confident about the interview. If they would just overlook the reason she'd been let go at her last job.

Driving back to the Cardone's, she couldn't help but think about Dante. In the last week, he'd become very irritated. He'd been very short and almost rude with her. She knew he was hurt and she tried everything to pull away from him, to spare him that hurt.

She looked at trying out for this job as her first steps away from a bad situation. When Kathleen had returned home from her week at the spa, Airlea had explained to her that things weren't working out, and it was time for her to look for another job.

Kathleen had tried to talk her out of leaving, but when it had come down to it, she'd understood Airlea's need to secure a future for herself.

She was just pulling into the long drive when she saw a man standing at the gate next to a large white truck. He waved at her and she stopped and rolled down her window a little, making sure the door was locked since the man was huge. His arms were easily as wide as her waist, and she could see his muscles bulge from under his t-shirt. She could see the muscles flex in his arms as he bent down to talk to her.

"Airlea Rossi?" She nodded her head and thought about hitting the gas if there was trouble.

"I'm Ethan Knight. I'm Katie's brother-in-law. She told me where to find you. I'd like to talk to you for a minute."

"Oh, yes." Airlea rolled her window down a little more. She remembered Jason talking to her about the man. He had been right, the man looked like he could easily snap someone in half.

"Would you care to come up to the house? We could talk…" She started.

"No, I'd better not. Miss Rossi, I believe your life is in danger." He blurted out.

She almost laughed. "I'm sorry?"

CHAPTER 13

*D*ante watched Airlea from across the dining room table and thought she looked different. He felt bad for treating her the way he had in the last few weeks since she'd left him alone that night. He'd been hurt. There was no other way to explain it.

He felt something for her, but he couldn't blame her. After all, they had entered the arrangement with an agreement that neither one of them was ready for a relationship. He'd been the one to break that. How was he supposed to know that he'd fall for her? But she was everything he wanted. Her kindness was beyond questionable. She was funny and easy to talk to. She was undeniably beautiful and at times he found himself just staring at her, dreaming about their future.

Maybe he was still mental from his accident or the pills he'd stopped taking a few weeks ago. He just couldn't stop thinking about her. When she'd driven into town earlier that day, he'd found himself watching out the window for her return. He knew he was crazy; he'd fallen for her so quickly. Hell, he'd only known her for two months. There was no way someone could or should fall for someone that fast.

Earlier his mother had told him that Airlea was in town for an interview. If she got this job, she'd leave, and he had to do something to get her to stay. Not only because he was not all the way healed, but because he just didn't want her to go. He looked at her again across the table and thought she looked nervous.

"How did your interview go today, Airlea?" He watched as she jumped at the mention of her name.

"Oh, it went fine."

"When will you know if you got the job?" His mother persisted in the questioning. He could tell Airlea was nervous and wanted to drop the subject.

"They said they would make a decision later this week." She took a large bite of bread and almost choked on the mouth full.

"Well, I know we'll be sorry to see you go, but I think if you could secure the position at the children's hospital, it would be wonderful for you."

"Thank you." She kept her head down and tried to eat her soup without another word.

"How did they handle the news of how you left your last job?" Dante just couldn't resist seeing her squirm. She looked up quickly and glared at him.

"Fine." She put her napkin down. "If you'll excuse me, I'm a little tired. I think I'll retire early. Good night."

She left the room and he watched her go. Not saying a word, he got up and walked from the room. He was still a lot slower than her, so when he reached her door, she had already shut it. He knocked on the door briefly, then entered without waiting for her to respond.

"What are you doing?" She covered herself with the shirt she'd just removed. He was pleased to see a bright white silk bra and instantly the desire flooded into him.

He kicked her door closed and flipped the lock. Without saying anything he walked over to her and pulled the shirt aside.

"Dante, I'm not in the mood." She tried to grab her shirt back. He held it out of her reach.

"So, this is what you look like in a bra." He smiled down at her. Her breasts looked fuller and higher. He enjoyed the look. Tossing her shirt on her bed, he reached up and lightly ran his hand across the mounds and watched her eyes go cloudy.

"I've decided to try everything I can to keep you here. Even if that means we just take our pleasures where we can." He said, then dipped his head and kissed the underside of her jaw moving downward until he licked the tops of her breast across the white lace.

"Dante." She whispered.

"Tell me you don't want this, that you don't want me, and I'll stop, I'll walk away." He said.

"No, don't." She shook her head.

"No, what?" He looked up at her.

"Don't stop." Her head rolled back, and he watched as her eyes close. Her hands came to his hair as she held him to her.

He knew he was fooling himself into believing that he'd take the pleasures as they came. He wanted more with her. He had to have more with her. His heart hurt when he thought about her leaving, but he knew he had to take what she'd give him and maybe find a way to persuade her to stay and give him another chance.

Airlea laid next to Dante and realized he'd maneuvered her. Since they were in her room, she couldn't get up and leave him. Short of kicking him out or being rude, she had no way of getting him to leave her bed. She lay there and listened to him breathing and felt his warm breath on her neck. She tried to fool herself into believing that she didn't enjoy the warmth or the feel of his skin on hers.

She didn't know what to do about the information she'd been given by Ethan earlier that evening. He'd told her that someone, a woman, in this house had hired the men who'd tried to kidnap Katie. He didn't know who yet, but he had found out that that person was now out to kill her. She had a good idea who it was.

It didn't really ease her mind knowing that Ethan was outside somewhere, watching the house. Watching out for her.

She did feel safer with Dante in the room, but she wished she could tell him what was happening. She had mixed feelings about the whole deal.

What had she done to deserve the woman's wrath? What had Katie done? The fact that she'd actually tried to kidnap her niece and hold her for ransom shocked her. It wasn't as if the woman was hurting for money. She lived in a big beautiful house and was given anything she asked for. Airlea didn't know all the details of the family fortune, but she knew that Florentina walked around like she ran the house.

She'd told Ethan her suspicions and had told him all that had happened to her since arriving. She'd mentioned Gino, the man who'd held her in the shed and how he had disappeared. Ethan took some more information from her about the man and told her he would try to find him. Maybe the man could shed some light on what had happened. And if need be, he could even help them corner Florentina.

Lying in the bed next to Dante in the dark, she watched the shadows cross the ceiling. As she was running through all of it in her head again, she heard a noise. At first, she thought it was coming from the hallway door, but then she turned her head and watched as the French doors slid open silently.

She froze; she knew she'd locked them. Dante was sprawled on his stomach, his face buried in her hair with his arm thrown over her chest.

"Airlea? It's Ethan." She relaxed and pulled the sheet up, so it covered her.

She didn't know how light a sleeper Dante was in normal circumstances, but she doubted he would sleep through the two of them chatting over him.

She pointed to the door and held up her finger, motioning that she'd be there in a minute.

After she watched Ethan walk silently back out the doors, she rolled out from under Dante and grabbed her bathrobe, then tiptoed to the door.

Closing it silently behind her, she looked around for Ethan. He was standing in the darkness, leaning against the wall. The cold in the night didn't seem to be affecting him.

"What's going on?" she whispered, walking towards him.

"I found Gino." He said.

She shivered thinking about the man who had attacked her. She didn't like him but knew he could possibly help tie up all the loose ends. "Did he tell you anything?"

"No, he's in a shallow grave about three hundred yards from here. Shot through the chest. Most likely at close range with a small caliber pistol." Ethan shook his head.

She was shocked and swayed a little thinking about it when Ethan grabbed her shoulders to help steady her, she heard Dante voice behind her.

"Get your hands off her." Her mind was too foggy to register the threatening tone, but Ethan did, and his hands dropped from her shoulders.

"I was just helping her." Ethan held up his hands and backed up a step. "You're Dante, Katie's brother? I'm Ethan Knight, her brother-in-law. Your brother-in-law, in a way."

"I don't care who you are. What are you doing here at midnight? Sneaking around? Airlea? What are you doing out here with him?" Dante moved closer.

"Dante…" How could she tell him? Maybe just blurting it out would be best? "Ethan is here to help find who tried to kidnap your sister. He's tracked the kidnapper's phone calls to this house. I think your aunt tried to kidnap Katie and has tried to kill me. She's the reason my brakes went out. I think she killed that man, Gino." She wrapped her arms around her chest and felt the night chill blow right through her.

"Airlea, it's freezing out here. Come inside and we can talk about this. Ethan?" Dante looked at the man. "Why don't you come in and we can discuss things further." Dante moved aside and let them by.

❄

The next morning just after breakfast, Airlea got a phone call. The children's hospital wanted to hire her. She'd actually gotten the job! Her mind had a list a mile long of things that needed to be done. She had to move all her stuff from the storage unit she'd placed everything in when she'd come here. She also needed an apartment.

But the one thing that hovered over all the others was Dante. He'd listened to everything Ethan had told him last night. He'd listened and had asked questions. She could see the sadness in his eyes when he'd finally accepted what they had been telling him.

She didn't know what the next steps were, but they had all agreed that she was better off moving out. Getting out of harm's way. He'd tried to argue with them, but once Dante had proof that it had been an attempt on her life, her brakes *had* been cut, he was determined that she not stay there any longer.

He'd even arranged for her to stay at his parents' place in Rome, which was a few blocks from her new job. She smiled and almost laughed. She had a new job! She knew she couldn't stay at the Cardone's apartment and spent the next day on the phone. By the end of the day, she had found three apartments to check out.

Dante wanted to go with her, for safety, but she finally persuaded him to stay home since the day would probably entail a lot of walking and he wasn't up to it yet. He'd checked her rental car before he allowed her to drive away and when everything looked fine, he'd kissed her right in front of his aunt who had stood on the back porch watching them.

Airlea signed a lease on the second apartment she looked at and went by her new job and talked to her boss. Her first day was Monday, but she wanted to stop by and drop off the paperwork he'd asked her for. He walked her around the complex and she got to see the state of the art therapy facility. There were almost a dozen kids in the large room, each one working in different areas with other therapists.

She couldn't wait to get back to what she loved to do. Her hands actually itched. Her mother arranged for all her belongings to be moved and they were going to be delivered to her new apartment the next day. Everything was moving very fast and she couldn't help but feel excited. This was the new start that she'd needed. Leaving all the bad behind her, she could only see good things for her future.

That night, Dante visited her room again. She'd locked her door, but he'd used a key he had to get in. She'd woken to him kissing her softly. She hadn't even heard him enter the room. She could tell he had mixed feelings about her leaving, but with everything up in the air with his aunt, she knew he felt better with her not being in harm's way.

The next day she met her mother in her new apartment. An hour later the truck arrived with all her furniture. It took only half an hour for the men to unload her possessions and the rest of the evening for her and her mother to unpack everything.

Her mother spent the night on the couch that night, and Airlea enjoyed having her around. It had been almost two months since she'd last seen her. She took after her mother in every way. And not just in looks; her mother was an emergency room nurse and was as independent as she was.

They ate breakfast out on her new patio and enjoyed watching people hustle by on the streets. They talked about the Cardone's and Airlea avoided talking about Dante. She could tell her mother was curious and knew something was up, but she didn't pressure her.

"Did I ever tell you that Damiano Cardone and I were engaged?"

Airlea almost choked on her tea. "No!"

"Yes, well, our families knew each other, and it was a somewhat arranged relationship." Her mother looked out over her balcony. "Well, I met Kathleen when she'd come to Rome a few years earlier. Well, we had stayed in contact after that. My parents had arranged a meeting with Damiano, but I was madly in love with your father at the time. On the day that I was set to meet Damiano, Kathleen called me and told me she was in town. So I set them up so I could run off to be with your father. I didn't know Kathleen was still married until after Dante was born. Life is funny, the choices you make can affect everything. Like you always say, everything is connected for a reason."

Airlea was so shocked, she didn't know what to say. She just looked across the table at her mother and tried to imagine the small twist of fate that had caused so many things to happen. Because of her mother, Kathleen had fallen for Damiano and cheated on her husband. But if she hadn't, Dante and Katie wouldn't have been born.

Her mother left before noon to head back home. It was nice having her live only two hours away again.

Airlea spent the rest of the day unpacking and moving

furniture around until everything looked just right. She kept playing her mother's conversation over and over.

That night she lay in her new apartment, in her very own bed, and felt relieved. She had done it. She had proven to herself that she could take care of herself after the huge blow of losing her job. Tomorrow she would start a new job, doing what she loved. She was very happy, but still, something was missing. She frowned and closed her eyes, telling herself that she didn't miss the warmth of Dante's arms around her.

CHAPTER 14

It took almost three months for things to come to a head. His aunt was not only sneaky; she was downright scary. Dante had worked with Ethan ever since that first night when he had met him.

Since the day after Airlea left, he'd borrowed the truck and had driven into town for his physical therapy appointments, not telling anyone that he met Ethan afterward and worked with him. They went through all his father's personal and business papers: the financial paperwork, the employee records, everything. There had to be a paper trail somewhere of what his aunt had done. Or was doing.

At first, Dante had questioned Ethan's tactics.

"Trust me, if your aunt paid anyone to do anything, there will be a trail."

Still, part of Dante's mind refused to believe that she was behind all this. He'd seen the mechanic's report from Airlea's car. Someone had used a pocket knife to cut both the main brake and her emergency brake lines. He couldn't deny that someone had wanted her brakes to fail. Plus, there was the whole Gino incident. The more he thought about what had happened, the more he questioned everything.

He kept his home life as normal as possible, not letting on that anything was wrong. He didn't even talk to his father about it.

He'd stopped by several times to see Airlea at her new job since her facility was just down the street from where his was. He enjoyed seeing her in her scrubs working with the small children. He'd even taken the time out to talk to a few older boys who had been in accidents. One of them had a metal bar around his lower leg, much like Dante's.

He had just gotten his bar and pins removed less than a week ago. It took some getting used to since he'd felt safer with the damn thing on. Now he felt exposed and worried about bumping his leg all the time.

After his last x-ray, the doctor said everything had healed up nicely. He would be keeping the four screws in his leg, but the ones in his shoulder would most likely need to be removed later on since they might end up giving him problems.

He was feeling steadier and walking with his full weight on his leg. If he focused as hard as he could, he didn't walk with a limp. He never did use the cane for walking. It had taken all of his patience to build up the muscles in that leg again. It still looked skinnier than the other one, but everyone assured him it was just in his mind. He had enjoyed being able to work out, doing his full regimen again. It felt good to be able to build himself up again.

He had even enrolled in school for the spring. He figured it would take until then to get everything in order.

When he told his father he was going back to school, his father had told him how proud he was. His mother had smiled and just patted his shoulder and said, "The college is just down the street from the children's hospital, isn't it?"

He'd laughed. He had asked both his parents not to tell his aunt what his plans were. Hopefully, his mother could keep her mouth shut until he figured everything out. They were sitting down for dinner one night when Rosa came into the room, looking scattered.

"Rosa? What's the matter?" his mother had asked.

"It's Airlea. That girl that worked here."

Dante almost dropped his fork. A million images flashed through his mind. He'd stepped back, thinking she would be safe if he stopped showing interest in her, but the truth was he'd put his heart on hold, waiting until he could go be with her. Now he thought about what he would do if she was taken away.

"What about her?" His mother almost stood out of her chair.

"She's – she's been arrested. It's on the news. They found all kinds of drugs in her apartment. They say she'd been stealing them."

His eyes flashed to his aunt's face and he watched in horror as she smiled a smile he'd never seen before. One he didn't even recognize.

"That is just bull." His mother stood all the way up and started walking towards the door.

"Mother?" Dante caught up with her. "Where are you going?"

"Well, isn't it obvious? I'm going to go bail her out.

Someone obviously set her up. There is no way that sweet young girl had anything to do with stealing drugs."

"Mom!" Dante pulled her to a stop. "We'll go together."

Airlea tried not to cry. Everything was ruined. She didn't know how those drugs got into her apartment, but she knew this time was different. They weren't found in her backpack and it wasn't just a few bottles. This time there were cases of high-dose drugs, the kind she'd only read about in school. Her mind had shut down when the police had shown up at her work. When they had slapped the handcuffs on her in front of the children and her co-workers, she had wanted to die.

When they had reached the police station, there had been reporters there and they had flashed pictures of her being led into the station. Someone had tipped them off, maybe the hospital. Why they cared about her was a mystery, but they had snapped the pictures like she was a movie star. Light bulbs flashed quickly, and she was almost blinded by the light. Then the police had finally told her what they had arrested her for, and her heart had sunk.

She had been fingerprinted, photographed, and searched, all of which had been beyond embarrassing. She didn't say a word except to answer simple questions. When they allowed her to make a phone call, she'd called her mother and told her what was happening. Her mother assured her she would be there as quickly as possible to post bail and they would work everything out.

She sat in the small room, her head resting against the cold brick wall, and cried.

Finally, Dante's aunt had made a mistake. Ethan watched the man leave Airlea's apartment and smiled while snapping the shutter on his camera. They had waited three months for this opportunity and he was almost done with this job. He quickly put his car in gear and followed the young man, knowing he would get the answers he needed from him easy enough.

He already had a few more jobs lined up, ones that he would charge for. This was family, and you didn't charge family. He watched the man get into the car and drive away.

Now he just needed to sit back and let things unfold so he could make everything right.

Dante smiled when he saw Airlea walk out of the double doors with her head hanging. His mother and father stood beside him. He watched as she looked up and realized it was them standing there. Her eyes found his first and he thought he saw fear and shame. He walked to her without the use of a crutch or cane and saw her smile slightly at his progress.

"Why are you here?" she asked, trying not to look at him.

"Airlea, we know you're innocent. We've come to bail you out. Besides, our mothers have talked and since your mom is still a good hour away, we told her we'd take you back to the house and meet her there."

"Dante, I can't drag your family into this." She said.

"Nonsense." His mother stepped forward and put a protective arm around her. "What kind of person would I be if I let an innocent girl rot in a cell for something she obviously didn't do?"

"Thank you, Mrs. Cardone," Airlea whispered.

"Kathleen." His mother insisted.

Airlea smiled a little and nodded her head, "Kathleen."

The car trip back to the house was a quiet one. Airlea sat with her back straight and looked out the side window. His mother chatted away about her recent trip to Portland to see Ric and Roberta. He was grateful his mother was someone who could hold a conversation with herself and fill the silence in the car. When they arrived, he noticed several police cars and watched Airlea tense.

"Don't worry. They aren't here for you," he whispered. He'd received a text from Ethan on the trip home and knew the final scene was about to unfold.

"What's this all about?" His father pulled into the driveway.

"Have we been robbed? Oh, I do hope nothing has happened to Florentina or Rosa." His mother and father rushed from the car.

"I'm sorry." Airlea sat in the car, not making a move to get out. "I'm not sure how he did it, but I think Angelo framed me again. I don't know how he got into my apartment."

"Airlea," he waited until she looked up at him. "It wasn't Angelo. It was my aunt. That's why they're here." They both watched as two female officers led his aunt from the house in handcuffs. His father stood there looking shocked, and his mother frantically tried to calm Rosa down as she cried into her apron.

They both watched as his aunt's eyes zeroed in on their car and when she saw Airlea sitting next to Dante, her eyes narrowed.

"Why does she hate me?" She whispered.

"Because she knows that I love you and I want to be with you." He said.

Airlea's eyes flew to his. "What?"

He smiled and got out of the car, then walked around and opened her car door. He pulled her gently towards a large olive tree near the side yard where there was a large stone bench. Sitting down next to her in the cool breeze he continued.

"It's been obvious to her even before it was to me. The night I gave you Nonna's watch." He pulled the watch case out of his pocket. He'd brought it along today, just in case she didn't agree to come back to the house with them.

"Open it and read the inscription." He motioned.

Airlea hesitated then took the watch from his fingers. When she opened it, she read out loud.

Hai il mio cuore per sempre

"You have my heart, forever." He translated. "That night I tried to give this to you, I just wanted to give something to you that was special. To show you how I felt. I didn't even remember the inscription. It wasn't until I put it back in the safe that I noticed it. I remembered Nonna telling me that one day, I would give this to the woman who had taken my heart. And on that day, I would know true happiness." He laughed, "She was, after all, part gypsy."

"Dante?"

"Airlea, I've been miserable for the last three months. First off, I need to get out of my parents' house. It's driving me crazy seeing them kissing everywhere. I can't even walk into the kitchen without seeing them together." She laughed, something he had hoped to hear. "I've bought a house just down the street from your apartment. Did I tell you that the children's hospital called, and you have your job back if you want it? They apologized for jumping to conclusions after they saw the proof that Ethan provided them. The photos clearly showed the man my aunt had hired and paid for out of her personal account plant those drugs in your apartment." He pulled her hand into his. "I've missed seeing you. I miss watching you eat across from me, seeing you every day, holding you at night. I know we both said we didn't want a relationship, and that this happened faster than we expected. But if you give this a chance, I think we can make this about more than just our pleasures. How about making it forever?"

"Dante, I've enjoyed the last three months, living in Rome." Part of him broke off and floated to the floor. "But there *has* been one thing I've been missing. You." She took his face into her hands and kissed him, just as the police car carrying his aunt drove by them.

Airlea watched as Dante walked towards her. It had been almost a year since she'd first walked in on him lying naked on his floor. He did walk with a slight limp, but so slight only his physical therapist would be able to see it.

It had been a few months since his aunt had finally confessed to killing his grandparents. Damiano had stood by his sister's side up to that point. After her confession, however, he had cut all ties and she was now sitting in a psych ward just outside of Rome, serving a life sentence for the death of her own parents. It had taken his family a while to adjust to all the news which had accounted for the delay in the wedding. Not to mention Dante had really wanted his brother to be there for the occasion. She smiled at the couple across the room who were busy smiling down at their new baby girl. Airlea stood next to Kathleen and Katie and smiled as Dante approached her with his hand out.

"May I have this dance?" He waited for her reply.

She looked at his mother first and when she just said, "Well, what are you waiting for?" Airlea laughed. Then she turned and looked at Katie.

"Don't look at me. I don't know if he can even dance." She chuckled. Reaching up, she put her hand into his and allowed him to pull her onto the dance floor.

The lights were dim, and the music was soft as he pulled her closer to him. Several other couples had joined them on the dance floor and started dancing near them. Katie and Jason, Kathleen and Damiano, and even Rick and Roberta holding their small daughter between them as they swayed to the music.

It felt so good to have his hands on her and to feel him close. He smiled, and she watched as his dimples flashed, then she looked into his eyes, and her steps faltered.

"Careful there, Mrs. Cardone. I'd hate to have to walk into my physical therapist's office on Monday and explain why I was walking with a new limp."

She smiled. "You could always tell her your new wife broke your other leg when you made fun of her dancing skills."

He laughed and then leaned down to place a soft kiss on her lips.

"Mmm, I think I can smooth talk her into forgiving me. Have I told you that I love you today?"

Airlea smiled. "We could get out of here and you could *show* your new wife just how much you love her."

He grabbed her hand and whisked her away towards the door while everyone in the room cheered.

SECRET GUARDIAN — PREVIEW

PROLOGUE

$\mathcal{E}$than had never cut it this close on a job before. His face and arms were covered in black paint. The black shirt and pants he wore were one of his standard uniforms, one he'd been wearing for as long as he could remember.

As he crouched down behind the small air conditioning unit next to the recently renovated house, he swore he'd never cut it this close again.

He watched as the four men argued over the small body. Was the kid still alive? Even though it wasn't part of his guarantee for the job, he hoped so.

He had less than five minutes before the final call that would decide the fate of the boy. It was now or never. Rushing from his position, he scaled the side wall in a blink of an eye, then quickly made it around the small house until he was standing at the back door. It took less than thirty seconds to open the locked door and even less time to make it to the end of the hallway. Since he was in all black, he doubted the four kidnappers could see him in the darkened room. He was standing just two feet away from them, in plain sight, as the men continued to argue.

The leader, a short, balding man by the name of Miles Collins, slammed his gun down on the table and told everyone to shut up. When the room was silent, Miles picked up a small cell phone from the table and dialed a number as he walked towards the back of the house. As he spoke, Ethan silently picked off each of the three remaining men.

He rushed behind the first and snapped his neck before the other two could respond. The second quietly went down with a quick punch to the throat. If Miles heard anything, it was only a quick intake of breath from the third man as Ethan's knife slid silently into his throat. Miles continued to talk on the phone as Ethan picked up his gun from the table and pointed it at the back of the man's head.

"Move and you're dead, just like your buddies."

Miles tensed as he held the phone up to his ear.

"Commander here, the room is secure," Ethan said to the room as Miles slowly dropped the phone to the floor in shock.

Just then, Ethan heard a small noise behind him. As he turned to check what it was, Miles spun around with his fist and clocked him on the side of his ear. Ethan didn't even blink, but just looked at the shorter man and slowly wiped the blood from his ear.

"You shouldn't have done that." Ethan used the butt of the gun to make a dent in the man's forehead. As the man hit the floor in a heap of unconscious bad guy, Ethan turned to see the eight-year-old boy lying on the table, staring at him like he was Superman.

"Are you a GI Joe?" the boy asked. Ethan chuckled and thought about it.

"Sure, kid. Let's get you home to your dad." He walked forward and lifted the small boy from the table and carried him out into the night.

CHAPTER 1

ive years later

Ann couldn't stand the man! How much more was she supposed to take? He was constantly late. Half the time he forgot his equipment. The rest of the time he was too busy checking himself in the mirror or flirting with her female staff to do his job properly.

But today was the absolute worst. He'd actually shown up to work with a scantily dressed Brazilian woman on each arm. Not to mention that he was over half an hour late.

They were in Brazil to cover the Carnival and most of her crew had enjoyed the festival. Even she'd even gone out last night and walked around, enjoying the sights, sounds, and food. Who wouldn't want to?

But seeing the two women plastering their naked bodies all over him this morning did something to her.

Nathan Cruz had only been working on her crew for three weeks. He'd been hired by her boss, Anthony, and when she'd complained about him, Anthony had just smirked and told her it was out of his hands. What did that even mean?

She'd had a problem with Nathan the minute she'd met him. He'd seemed so self-absorbed and huge. The man had arms the size of elephant trunks, and his neck was as thick as her thighs. Ann had known many men like him; self-absorbed, every one of them.

He probably spent more time at a gym than he did watching the news or learning about what was going on in the world. You needed to be up on current events if you wanted to stay working for one of the top media outlets. Of course, the man was just behind the camera. She supposed the extra muscles came in handy when it came time to lug all that heavy equipment around.

Her last cameramen, Albert, had been a short, frail-looking older man. She and the two other guys in her four-man crew, Joe, and Mark, had always had to help him unload the equipment.

But as she, Joe, and Mark stood around waiting for Nathan, she decided what needed to be done. When they made it back to Austin, she was going to make it her mission to see that Nathan got his pink slip.

It wasn't as if she was a tyrant. She'd even bought the whole crew drinks their first night in Brazil. She tried to enjoy herself around the three men. Joe and Mark had been on her crew for a few years and she felt somewhat comfortable around them. But with Nathan there, she just couldn't seem to loosen up.

She thought he was very attractive, so maybe that had

a lot to do with it. The sexual tension was always a good reason to be nervous around someone. But with him, it was more. She couldn't explain it, but it was almost as if he went out of his way to piss her off.

That first night, he'd only drunk one beer and the rest of the evening had just sat around flirting with any woman that walked by, which happened to be a lot of women. He flirted with everyone except her.

Maybe that was it. She was used to getting hit on by coworkers, especially attractive ones. But Nathan went out of his way not to hit on her, which made her believe that he had something against her. Or that he was flirting with other women to see her reaction. Whatever it was, she wasn't buying his act. At least she thought it was an act.

Now as he approached the van, he had a wicked smile plastered on his face. She crossed her arms and grinned back, thinking about getting him fired.

"Sorry I'm late, boss. I found these two and we got to talking." She watched as the women blushed.

Yeah, I bet they were just talking, Ann thought.

"We had to carry all your gear out here ourselves. You owe Joe and Mark an apology."

He walked over and gave Mark a high five. One of the women walked over and gave Joe a kiss on his cheek, making the older man blush.

She realized that they were pretty much ignoring her, and she felt like she was just being a nagging woman.

They'd been in Brazil for over a week covering the festivals, and she'd had enough of all three of them. Somehow Nathan had gotten closer to Mark and Joe in the last week than she had in the last three years, which made her feel extremely annoyed and hurt.

As everyone piled in the van, she watched as the two young women tried to get in. She held her arm over the door and blocked them, looking over to Nathan.

"They can't come along." She had yet to understand his expressions; his hazel eyes hid his emotions too well. But right now, she assumed he was annoyed.

"She's right, girls," he said. She heard the standard pouting objections from both women who turned and kissed him one after another, then walked away.

Finally, they got in the van and headed out. Now they were late for the meeting with her source, whom she hadn't told her crew about. Everyone was still under the impression that they were meeting Isabella Torres, this year's Carnival Queen.

"Where did you say this meeting was?" Joe asked as he drove the narrow side streets. Ann gave him directions and once the van started climbing the hills towards the slums, everyone got very quiet.

Finally, Mark leaned forward and asked, "Ann, are you going to tell us why we are meeting the queen of the carnival up here in the favelas?"

"We aren't." She sat forward in her seat as she felt the thrill and excitement of disobeying her boss set in.

"What exactly are we doing up here, then?" Joe asked while keeping his eyes on the ever-narrowing streets.

"We are meeting a man about a job." She knew she was being vague, but she didn't want anyone to chicken out. Especially since she knew the story could earn her world recognition, and possibly even the Pulitzer.

"Tell me this isn't another scheme to get a Pulitzer." Joe looked over at her.

She waited to answer them until they pulled in front of

a small, brightly colored yellow building. Laundry hung from wires and ropes across the entrance of the alleyway. There were brightly colored designs on the houses that she knew marked each house and its occupant's loyalties to a particular drug lord.

Heitor, her source, was standing in the doorway, looking a little nervous. She'd met him late last night while she'd been enjoying the carnival. She'd just stepped out after dealing with Nathan when a large Brazilian man had approached her. He was an older man and at first, he'd scared her, since he'd approached her from behind. He'd tried to pull her into the alleyway by her arm, and when she'd resisted, he'd told her that he knew she was a journalist, that he'd been watching her at her hotel as she covered the carnival. At first, she'd shivered, thinking that someone had followed her, watched her. Then he'd gone into quick detail about what he did and who he worked for. Nathan had stepped out of the hotel and had started walking towards them, so she'd arranged to meet him today. He'd pushed a piece of paper into her hand with the address and directions to the meeting after he'd told her the time.

She'd asked if he would be willing to go on camera with his story, but he'd shaken his head and left quickly as Nathan had approached her. He'd acted like she'd been in trouble, but she just laughed at him and tried to have a good time getting lost in the crowd.

She didn't know why Heitor wanted the interview. She was sure he must have been marked for death already for him to take such a bold step.

"Heitor, I'm sorry we're late." She glared in Nathan's direction. "We can be set up in under five minutes."

"I'm sorry, miss, I thought you were coming alone. I've changed my mind about talking to you." The man's eyes were darting in every direction, taking in her crew. She noticed his hands shaking and realized she had to do something quickly or she was going to lose the interview.

"Heitor, why don't you and I go inside and talk."

It took her the whole five minutes that her crew was setting up to calm him down and convince him that he'd be perfectly safe. There was no way anyone would know it was him on the camera.

As the interview got started, she pulled out the list of questions she'd worked up earlier that morning. She knew how to work an interview. She started with some easy questions to make him feel relaxed, then she built up to some harder questions, and finally she asked the doozy of all questions.

Heitor was true to his word. He answered every question about his boss and his ties to the police, giving her details on how much money was involved. But most importantly, he had information on the connections between his boss, the police, and a local politician. This was the scoop she was digging for.

A chamber deputy, a judiciary, and a Supreme Court justice were all in the pockets of one or more drug lords, or worse, they were the ones in control. Heitor didn't have that last piece of information that would have tied it all up nicely.

When he talked about the connections, he stuttered and became very agitated. Ann could tell he knew more, but before she could get names and more details, Joe pulled her aside.

"Ann, we need to leave. I think you have enough," he

said. "Can I talk to you?" He motioned towards the doorway.

She looked at him for a few seconds, then followed him out front. "I'll be right back, Heitor."

The man nodded and looked even more afraid.

The second she stepped out the small opening, Joe turned on her.

"How dare you!" His face was red and she noticed sweat running down his neck. She'd never seen him look so upset.

"How dare you put your crew at risk like this. I mean, we come down here, flashing our press badges all over the place. Then you get wind of this." He motioned towards the small box of a home. "You didn't even bring your crew in on the secret. Just plow right through, as if you're the queen of TV. Did you think of our safety? Or that of the man in there, beyond this interview? I mean, look around!" He motioned to the courtyard. Their large white van sat in front of the row of huts that were falling down, a white beacon in a sea of trash. "You may have covered his face, but can you cover the fact that now everyone within a one-mile radius knows that the man sitting inside talked to the press?"

She smiled, "Relax, Joe. This isn't his place. You see that symbol there?" She pointed to the small patch of bright colors.

When Joe nodded, she continued, "That's the sign of the Red Command. Earlier this year the police seized control of this whole area. They are in control here, not the drug lords."

She crossed her arms as she watched Joe look around and notice the small children playing in the streets. There were women and old men sitting outside like they were enjoying a day at the beach. You wouldn't see that if the drug lords still controlled this section. Smiling, she walked back into the room only to find Nathan and Mark sitting in the darkened room alone.

"Where is Heitor?"

Nathan shrugged his shoulders and continued to play with his camera. Mark pointed to a doorway. "He said he needed a bathroom break."

Ann rushed towards the opening and realized it was a back door. "Great! Can't you two keep your eyes on someone for five minutes?" She turned and glared at the men. "Well, I guess the interview is over now, anyway," she said to Joe who had just walked in. "Pack it up, boys." She chewed her bottom lip, hoping she had gotten enough in the interview.

It seemed to take longer to get back down the hill to their hotel. The carnival was in full swing since it was the next to last evening. She wanted to work with Mark and get everything edited and sent to Austin before sundown.

The two of them sat in the hot van and worked for almost three hours. Finally, just before the sunset, when she was fully satisfied with the outcome, she grabbed the burned DVD of the footage and started back up to her room to call her boss.

She was halfway down the hall when Nathan came rushing out of Joe's room. He grabbed her arm and pulled her into what appeared to be a closet.

"What—?" She couldn't get another word out, as his big hand clamped over her mouth. His muscular arms held her tight and the look in his eyes told her she'd better stay quiet. Then she heard the loud noises. They seemed to go on forever. Nathan pulled her down past a few shelves until, finally, they were crouched on the floor behind a large row of toilet paper and towels. His full weight was on her, crushing her to the hard ground. His hand was still over her mouth, blocking out any protest she had.

Then there was an explosion and she watched in horror as the door was ripped off the hinges. A large fireball came rushing towards them. She tried to scream just before a large chunk of wood hit her head and everything went black.

This is a work of fiction. Names, characters, places, and incidents either are the product of the author's imagination or are used fictitiously, and any resemblance to actual persons, living or dead, business establishments, events or locales is entirely coincidental.

SECRET PLEASURE

DIGITAL ISBN: 978-1-942896-34-0

PRINT ISBN: 978-1-942896-35-7

Copyeditor: Erica Ellis – inkdeepediting.com

The Pride Series

Finding Pride

Discovering Pride

Returning Pride

Lasting Pride

Serving Pride

Red Hot Christmas

My Sweet Valentine

Return To Me

Rescue Me

The Secret Series

Secret Seduction

Secret Pleasure

Secret Guardian

Secret Passions

Secret Identity

Secret Sauce

The West Series

Loving Lauren

Taming Alex

Holding Haley

Missy's Moment

Breaking Travis

Roping Ryan

Wild Bride

Corey's Catch

Tessa's Turn

The Grayton Series

Last Resort

Someday Beach

Rip Current

In Too Deep

Swept Away

High Tide

Lucky Series

Unlucky In Love

Sweet Resolve

Best of Luck

A Little Luck

Silver Cove Series

Silver Lining

French Kiss

Happy Accident

Hidden Charm

A Silver Cove Christmas

Entangled Series – Paranormal Romance

The Awakening

The Beckoning

The Ascension

Haven, Montana Series

Closer to You

Never Let Go

Holding On

Pride Oregon Series

A Dash of Love

My Kind of Love

Season of Love

Tis the Season

Dare to Love

Where I Belong

Wildflowers Series

Summer Nights

Summer Heat

Stand Alone Books

Twisted Rock

For a complete list of books:

http://JillSanders.com

Jill Sanders is a New York Times, USA Today, and international bestselling author of Sweet Contemporary Romance, Romantic Suspense, Western Romance, and Paranormal Romance novels. With over 55 books in eleven series, translations into several different languages, and audiobooks there's plenty to choose from. Look for Jill's bestselling stories wherever romance books are sold or visit her at jillsanders.com

Jill comes from a large family with six siblings, including an identical twin. She was raised in the Pacific Northwest and later relocated to Colorado for college and a successful IT career before discovering her talent for writing sweet and sexy page-turners. After Colorado, she decided to move south, living in Texas and now making her home along the Emerald Coast of Florida. You will find that the settings of several of her series are inspired by her time spent living in these areas. She has two sons and off-set the testosterone in her house by adopting three furry little ladies that provide her company while she's locked in her writing cave. She enjoys heading to the beach, hiking, swimming, wine-tasting, and pickleball with her husband, and of course writing. If you have read any of her books, you may also notice that there is a love of food, especially sweets! She has been blamed for a few added pounds by her assistant, editor, and fans... donuts or pie anyone?

facebook.com/JillSandersBooks

twitter.com/JillMSanders

bookbub.com/authors/jill-sanders